READY TO DRAW

Ross turned abruptly, and saw the two men he had seen in town at the restaurant—Kerb Dahl and the shorter, hard-faced man.

In that single instant he became aware of many things. Bob Vernon stood in the door, white as death. Kerb Dahl, a hard gleam in his eyes, was on the right and he walked with elbows bent, hands swinging at his gun butts.

Behind Ross there was a low moan of fear from Sherry, but he did not move, only waited and watched the two men coming toward him. It could be here. It could be now. It could be at this moment.

Dahl spoke first, his lean, cadaverous face hard and with a curiously set expression. The shorter man had moved apart from him a little. Haney remembered the girl behind him, and knew he dare not fight—but some sixth sense warned him that somewhere else would be a third man, probably with a rifle. The difference.

Kerb Dahl spoke. "You're Ross Haney. I reckon you know me. I'm Dahl, an' this here is the first time you've come to the VV, an' this is goin' to be the last. You come on this place again an' you get killed. We don't aim to have no troublemakers around."

Ross Haney held very still, weighing his next words carefully. This could break into a shooting match in one instant….

Other books by Louis L'Amour:

THE GOLDEN WEST (Anthology)
THE UNTAMED WEST (Anthology)

The Sixth Shotgun

Published by AmazonEncore
P.O. Box 400818
Las Vegas, NV 89140

ISBN-13: 9781477831526
ISBN-10: 1477831525

This title was previously published by Dorchester Publishing; this version has been reproduced from the Dorchester book archive files.

LOUIS L'AMOUR

THE SIXTH SHOTGUN

TABLE OF CONTENTS

Foreword

by Jon Tuska

It is this by which we measure a
man, by what he does with his life,
by what he creates to leave behind.
—Louis L'Amour

When Louis L'Amour died on June 19, 1988, he was the most decorated author in the history of American letters. In 1983 he was the first American author ever to be awarded a Special National Gold Medal by the United States Congress for lifetime literary achievement and in 1984 President Reagan awarded him the Medal of Freedom, the highest civilian honor in the nation.

L'Amour for decades had merchandised himself as much as, and even more than, his Western fiction with a success enjoyed by no one since Ned Buntline who had made Buffalo Bill Cody a figure of international prominence. Movie cowboy Tim McCoy, who knew Buffalo Bill, recalled him as once saying that so much had been written about him and his various exploits that he no longer knew himself what was true and what may have been exaggeration. L'Amour had no such publicist as Buntline; instead, he was the principal source of information about his past. In a letter quoted in the

Gregg Press' reprint edition of KILKENNY (1954), L'Amour claimed to have been taught to use a six-shooter by Bill Tilghman, a frontier lawman noted for having captured Bill Doolin and who was shot to death in 1924 at the age of seventy-one by a drunken Prohibition agent when Tilghman was city marshal at Cromwell, Oklahoma.

He was born Louis Dearborn LaMoore on March 22, 1908 in Jamestown, North Dakota, the son of Louis Charles LaMoore and Emily Lavisa Dearborn LaMoore, the youngest of seven children. The main source of biographical information about L'Amour while he was alive came from the brief sketches that he supplied and periodically revised on the back pages of his original paperback novels. He contended that he ran away from home at fifteen and for at least two decades traveled throughout the world having the kinds of adventures he would later describe in his fiction. Among the jobs he said he had were those of ranch hand, merchant seaman, roustabout for a traveling circus, fruit picker, ship loader, and lumberjack. He recalled being very athletic, bicycling through Italy, Hungary, and British India, fighting as he traveled, eventually becoming a professional boxer. Depending on which one of these sketches you might read, L'Amour won anywhere from fifty-one to fifty-eight of fifty-nine bouts. While in Macao in 1927, L'Amour claimed he heard a story about a sunken ship and was determined to be the first one to salvage the money left in the captain's safe. He was the first and, afterward, went to live a Bohemian life in Paris. Wearying finally of being a drifter and loner for so long, L'Amour said he returned to the United States in the late 1930s and turned to writing fiction for pulp magazines, turning out mysteries and detective stories, adventure tales, sports stories, and Westerns. His first book was a collection of verse titled SMOKE FROM THIS ALTAR (1939), printed in a very limited edition by a publisher in Oklahoma City. During the Second World War, L'Amour served in a tank destroyer unit and in the Transportation Corps. It was not until after the war that he came to specialize in writing Western fiction for the pulp magazines.

"The cowards didn't go," L'Amour remarked as we sat across from each other in the summer of 1980 on the patio behind his large, Spanish-style home on the corner of Sunset Boulevard and Loring Avenue in Los Angeles. "It was inevitable that the Indian way of life should cease. And look at what replaced it! Where there was wilderness, there are now hospitals and schools."

"And what of the buffalo?" I asked him.

"They had outlived their usefulness," he replied confidently. "It was necessary that they be killed. Now there are farms throughout that whole area, farms that grow food to feed one third of the world. It's a matter of progress. The Indians didn't own the lands they occupied. Many of the tribes, in fact, had only recently occupied certain regions before the white man arrived. The Indians took the land from others, the cliff dwellers, for example. And the white man took the land from the Indians. It wasn't the Indians' land to claim or to sell. It went to the strongest. The white men were stronger. There's nothing more stupid, in my opinion, than to talk about paying the Indians for the land. It was never theirs to sell."

The garden beyond the patio was neatly manicured, a truly Wordsworthian garden, Nature cut back, trimmed and controlled. A seemingly endless stream of cars swished past on Sunset Boulevard and the sky was tinted by a reddish-brown smog.

"My favorite tree," L'Amour continued, "is the white aspen. For me, it is the most beautiful tree in all Nature. I saw a terrible thing on a recent trip I took. I climbed to the top of this hill and I could see white aspen covering an adjacent hill. But growing around the bottoms of those white aspens was scrub oak. Scrub oak is short, tough. It will choke the life out of the white aspens. That's the way it is in Nature."

L'Amour then took me on a tour of that part of the house in which he worked, the library with its 10,000 volumes stored in gigantic bookcases that could swing out into the room only to reveal a second built-in bookcase of similar dimension, all of them filled from top to bottom with books, most of them pertaining to some aspect of the American West.

"I use these books in my research," L'Amour explained. "Every incident in any story I write is authentic and usually based either on something I personally experienced or something that happened in history. And over here"—he said, moving toward a map case in the hallway—"are my maps." He pulled open a drawer to show a thick pile of topographical maps. Handing me one to study, he pointed out the extensive detail in the cartography. "When I say there is a rock in the road in one of my books, my readers know that, if they go to that spot and look, they'll find that rock."

"There is one thing that continues to trouble me about your books," I said.

"And what is that?"

"Well, take LAST STAND AT PAPAGO WELLS. After an Indian attack, according to the story, only five characters have been killed, but one of the surviving characters counts six corpses."

"I'll have to go back and count them again," L'Amour said, and smiled. "But, you know, I don't think the people who read my books would really care."

It was a curious remark and very much at odds with the impression he had been trying to give me when showing me his library and his detailed maps. Even the way he dressed, with the striped cowboy shirt, the silver belt buckle, the Western boots and rawhide bolo tie was intended to give one the impression that he was a man who had stepped out of the 19th Century into the 20th.

"If you want to know about the way the West was, and if you want to know about me," he said with emphasis, "you're going to have to read my books, as many of them as you can. It'll become clearer to you that way, rather than by anything I might tell you here today."

Very early in his career as a pulp writer, in the period just prior to the outbreak of the Second World War, L'Amour created a series character named Pongo Jim Mayo, the master of a tramp steamer in Far Eastern waters, in L'Amour's words "an Irish-American who had served his first five years at sea sailing out of Liverpool and along the west coast of Africa's Pongo River, where he picked up his nickname. He's a character I created from having gotten to know men just like him while I was a seaman in my yondering days." After the war, when L'Amour began to specialize in Western fiction, he wrote most frequently under the pseudonym Jim Mayo, taking it from this early fictional character. One of L'Amour's earliest series characters in his Western fiction was the gunfighter, Lance Kilkenny, who figured in two of his early pulp short novels. "The Rider of Lost Creek" by Jim Mayo appeared in *West* (4/47). It was expanded somewhat when it reappeared as a Bantam original paperback in 1976. L'Amour in all his Western novels had actually a very limited number of plots that he would use over and over again and, of course, he borrowed incidents and episodes from this story or that for re-use.

"The Rider of Lost Creek" employs what I would call L'Amour's range war plot. The first chapter is given over to establishing Lance Kilkenny's mode of operation—that he is the fastest gun in the West, that once there is a gunfight he leaves the district right after it is over, and that very little is known about him, even what he looks like. One day some time back Mort Davis saved Kilkenny's life after he was shot up and now Davis has sent out word that he needs Kilkenny's help. Mort has filed a claim on a water hole near Lost Creek in the Live Oak country. The district is dominated by two wealthy cattlemen, Webb Steele and Chet Lord, and both are at loggerheads, each one claiming for himself the water hole that Davis occupies. There is a master villain, Royal Barnes, who is masquerading as an Easterner. He has a secret cabin in Apple Canyon just above the saloon operated by heroine Nita Riordan and her bodyguard, Jaime Brigo. Barnes is responsible for stirring up the trouble between Steele and Lord, figuring they will kill each other off so he can claim both their ranches. There is also a mad-dog killer loose in the district and there have been a number of murders over the years. Barnes is not the murderer, but rather Steve Lord, Chet Lord's crazy son. Kilkenny enters the fracas, meets and falls in reciprocal love with Nita at first sight, and then works to get Steele and Lord to realize that they are pawns in a bigger game. The Brockman brothers, Abel and Cain, are among the renegades working for Barnes. Kilkenny manages to gun Abel while only knocking Cain unconscious. Cain seeks revenge against Kilkenny in a fist fight in which he is beaten into submission. As many of L'Amour's heroes, Lance's prowess is due to his having done some boxing in the past. There are the typical L'Amour errors of construction in the story. In one scene a scarred cowpuncher is a Lord rider for his first piece of dialogue and the next time he speaks he is identified as a Steele hand. As is the case with most of L'Amour's heroes—and as he claimed about himself—Lance Kilkenny is a self-created man. When Nita inquires about his parents, Lance asks: " 'Does it matter? No man is anything but what he makes of himself, I suspect, although no doubt the inheritance is there. It is what he does with what he was given that matters. . . .'" There is also the most common L'Amour theme of all, the new home theme, as we are told that for Kilkenny "it was the longing of a lonely man for a home, a fireside, for the nearness of a woman and the laughter of children. For someone to work for, to protect, someone to belong to, and some place where you fitted in." Chet Lord tells Kilkenny the sad truth about his son when he is dying of natural causes. Steve Lord is killed by a hidden spring gun when trying to enter Barnes's secret cabin, and Kilkenny goes up against Barnes despite raw hands from the fight with Cain Brockman. Kilkenny kills Barnes but is wounded and Nita helps nurse him back to health. At the end, Lance rides off to think things over, to determine if he dares to marry in view of his reputation as a gunfighter.

This story, as all of L'Amour's magazine fiction from the 1940s and 1950s, was copyrighted through the composite copyright in the issue registered in the name of the magazine publishing company. Under the Copyright Act of 1909, the law then in force, the only way an author could claim ownership in a story appearing in a magazine was to request an assignment of the story in his name out of the composite copyright in the issue, endorsed by the magazine publishing company, and to record it separately in the assignment files at the Copyright Office. Every copyright then had to be renewed in the twenty-eighth year after registration of the original copyright, either by the author or by his successor-in-interest. L'Amour made no effort to get these necessary assignments. Even stories published in a slick magazine like *The Saturday Evening Post* were forgotten. For example, the short story, "Booty for a Badman", a Tell Sackett story originally published in *The Saturday Evening Post* (7/30/60), was renewed by the magazine publishing company in the composite copyright for the issue because L'Amour had never secured an assignment for the story. This allowed the new *The Saturday Evening Post* to run the story as a two-part serial, beginning with the issue dated September, 1988, without paying the author anything for reprinting it. Most of the pulp magazine publishers ceased doing business in the 1950s and, unlike *The Saturday Evening Post*, few of them, or their successors-in-interest, bothered to renew the composite copyrights in the issues in the twenty-eighth year. It is due to this singular carelessness in protecting his copyrights that virtually all of L'Amour's magazine fiction, including stories that he later reworked into expanded paperback novels, are now in the Public Domain. When, in the 1980s, while L'Amour was still alive, Carroll & Graf began publishing L'Amour's Public Domain fiction in book collections, L'Amour and Bantam Books brought suit for infringement of copyright, only for the case to be decided in favor of Carroll & Graf since the material was in the Public Domain and could be reprinted by anyone with a mind to do so. To counteract any effort by publishers from reprinting this fiction, L'Amour countered with a series of special reprint paperbacks issued by Bantam Books of all his Public Domain fiction, declaring these books to be the "authorized" versions, but nothing else could really be done about the matter, any more than any other author or author's heirs can make any valid claim to any work now in the Public Domain.

"A Man Called Trent" by Jim Mayo appeared in *West* (12/47). When it was reissued in an "authorized" edition in 1986, L'Amour commented in an Author's Note that "such people as Jared Tetlow in this story are all too familiar." Apparently L'Amour had not re-read the short novel before he submitted it for reprint since Jared Tetlow is not the villain in this story, but rather is a character in the final story in the Kilkenny series, KILKENNY, first published as an original paperback by Ace in 1954. Because L'Amour had reworked "A Man Called Trent" into THE MOUNTAIN VALLEY WAR, published as a paperback original by Bantam in 1978, years before the original story, by then in the Public Domain, was reprinted, it is instructive, I think, to go into some detail concerning the plot of the original in order to contrast it with the rewrite. In fact, "A Man Called Trent" is one of the finest Western stories L'Amour would ever write. The basic storyline is the one variation L'Amour contrived for the range war plot. The setting is New Mexico, but all of the places and names came from L'Amour's imagination. The short novel opens to a nester named Dick Moffitt lying dead where he was killed by King Bill Hale's riders. Sally Crane, who is sixteen and was adopted by Moffitt, and Moffitt's fourteen-year-old son Jack witnessed Moffitt's murder from hiding, and then went to a cabin owned by a man named Trent for safety.

Kilkenny in this story has taken the name of Trent, hoping to escape his reputation as a gunfighter. King Bill Hale has decided that he wants the graze in the high country for his cattle and to get it he must drive out the nesters. Cub Hale, King Bill's son, is a killer who has been running rough-shod ever since he became old enough to carry a gun. Heroine Nita Riordan owns the Crystal Palace in Cedar Bluff where she is protected by her half-Yaqui bodyguard, Jaime Brigo. King Bill Hale wants Nita to marry him, but she is holding out for Lance Kilkenny, hoping he eventually will overcome his scruples about leaving her a young widow. Kilkenny joins forces with the other nesters. When a storekeeper in Cedar Bluffs refuses to sell supplies to the nesters, Kilkenny tells him: "'This is America, an' here the people always win. Maybe not at first, but they always win in the end.'" This is a theme that would figure prominently in all of L'Amour's subsequent Western fiction. In L'Amour's West, the people always do win. But they do not win by themselves. They win because the L'Amour hero shows them the way and because they can work with the L'Amour hero. The most interesting group among the nesters is the Hatfield clan, headed up by Parson Hatfield. The Hatfields are from Kentucky and obviously constituted the germinal idea from which, later, the Sacketts would grow in that saga of many volumes. Kilkenny makes an attempt to restore peace by confronting King Bill Hale at Hale's saloon in town. The attempt results in a bloody fist fight in which King Bill is left in a heap on the floor. It is known that King Bill has been planning a celebration in Cedar Bluff to mark his first ten years in the district, and, after this beating, he decides to import a professional prize fighter named Tombull Turner to go up against Kilkenny in the ring. Kilkenny accepts the challenge because it will provide the only chance for him to communicate with officials from Santa Fe who have been invited to attend. Kilkenny "knew how men of all sorts and kinds admire a fighting man. The Santa Fe officials, especially if one of them was Halloran, would be no exception. He would be going into the fight as an underdog. Hale wanted him whipped, but King Bill's power was destroying his shrewdness."

Four of the nesters take a wagon to the nearby town of Blazer to get supplies denied them in Cedar Bluff, and Kilkenny, by taking a wagon directly across the Smoky Desert, hopes to reach Blazer at the same time or a little ahead of them. Some of the best descriptive writing L'Amour would ever do is to be found in his handling of Kilkenny's trek across the wasteland. When Kilkenny arrives in Blazer, a tough named Gaddis is seen to enter a saloon wearing Jody Miller's gun. Jody Miller was one of the nesters in the nester wagon. Kilkenny enters the saloon and begins a conversation with Gaddis, claiming that he recognizes him from the gun he is wearing. Calling Gaddis by the name Jody Miller, Kilkenny recalls where he first saw Jody and how Jody knows Halloran at the state capital. The bluff works. It throws the renegades in the saloon off balance and several of them are gunned down in the ensuing fight. Once back at the Hatfield place, Kilkenny insists that his way is best. He wants to fight Turner and talk to Halloran during the bout. In the meantime, Kilkenny learns that Cain Brockman, from the earlier story, has arrived in Cedar Bluff, determined to kill him. Kilkenny manages to persuade Cain to hold off until after the fight. The fight takes place and Kilkenny does talk to Halloran from the ring between clinches and body blows. Kilkenny wins and Halloran warns King Bill that, if Kilkenny's charges are true, King Bill will be tried and hanged. This is the beginning of the end for King Bill. Some of his hands see the writing on the wall, run off with a herd of his cattle, and Cub Hale takes off after them with some hardcases still loyal to the brand. In despair, King Bill shoots himself. When Cub Hale and the hardcases return, Cub sends the hardcases to kidnap Nita, but Kilkenny outwits them and they are captured. The final confrontation is the shoot-out between Kilkenny and Cub Hale.

In L'Amour's rewritten expansion of this story, all the bad traits of the later L'Amour are unfortunately evident. To begin with, there is the strident L'Amour rhetoric. On the way to the Hatfield place, Kilkenny tells young Sally Crane and Jack Moffitt that "'the Hatfields know who they are, they know what they believe in, and their kind will last. Other kinds of people will come and go. The glib and confident, and whiners and complainers, and the people without loyalty, they will disappear, but the Hatfields will still be there plowing the land, planting crops, doing the hard work of the world because it is here to be done. Consider yourself fortunate to know them.'" The reader is not informed, however, if the youngsters are suitably impressed.

The first Dell Books paperbacks provided maps on the back cover that a reader could consult while reading the story, whether it be a detective story, a Western, or some other kind of fiction. L'Amour during his final decade put this idea to his own purposes, providing maps at the beginnings of his novels to show a reader where the action supposedly took place. Since no such place names could be found in New Mexico, for THE MOUNTAIN VALLEY WAR L'Amour changed the location of the story to a "remote corner of southwestern Idaho." The name Smoky Desert was retained, but it was said to be only a local and not very well-known designation for an area defined on the map as rough lands. A footnote about actual boxing matches in the 19th Century was added to provide a flavor of authenticity to Kilkenny's fight with Turner. By far the most damaging changes were the ways in which L'Amour destroyed the integrity of his plot. When Kilkenny enters the saloon in Blazer and confronts Gaddis and the other renegades, taking Gaddis for Jody Miller and stating that Jody knows Halloran at the state capital, it is no longer a bluff but an actual statement of fact. Hence, when Kilkenny bends Halloran's ear during the boxing match, King Bill tries to throw Halloran off by calling Jody Miller "trash" only for Halloran to reply: "'Jody Miller . . . was married to my sister. He was as likely a young man as I know. And as honest.'" This remark makes the whole fight sequence and the conclusion of the novel superfluous. All that needed to happen was for Jody Miller's widow to come to town to see her brother, or even just write Halloran a letter, and King Bill Hale's reign of terror would have been over before it had really begun!

When I was at work on his entry for the ENCYCLOPEDIA OF FRONTIER AND WESTERN FICTION (1983), I had compared the texts of L'Amour's pulp stories with his later expansions of them and asked him why he had made many of the changes he did. He replied that the reason he felt it was necessary to make such sweeping alterations in expanding these short novels into the "new" book-length novels to be published by Bantam was that he feared the original stories were still under copyright by the owners of the magazines and he wanted to avoid any claims of copyright infringement from them. This, of course, was stated before the copyright infringement lawsuit that he and Bantam brought against Carroll & Graf during the course of which L'Amour discovered, to his dismay, that the magazine copyrights had never been renewed and that, indeed, no one could any longer claim proprietary ownership in the original magazine stories.

The Kilkenny trilogy concludes with KILKENNY. The plot of this novel is essentially the same range war plot variation as that to be found in "A Man Called Trent" with one difference: Instead of the villain's being a rancher indigenous to the district, as was King Bill Hale, Jared Tetlow with his giant herds of cattle comes to the district intent on driving out all the other ranchers so he can carve out an empire for himself. Included among these other ranchers is heroine Nita Riordan, still with her faithful bodyguard, Jaime Brigo, and still hoping Lance Kilkenny will come to her. She is what the Romans called *univera*, as are most L'Amour heroines, since "her childhood training, her father, all her background conditioned her to love for one man only." Kilkenny has homesteaded in the district, again using the name Trent in order to elude his reputation. This is early L'Amour, when he was against the big ranchers, before the Sacketts who would become empire builders themselves with L'Amour's total endorsement. "Kilkenny's sympathies were with the small ranchers, the men who were building homes rather than empires. For one man to grow so large as Tetlow meant many men must remain small or have nothing. The proper level lay between the two extremes, and this was the American way." Kilkenny joins forces with the small ranchers and townspeople opposing Tetlow's take over. We learn one more thing, in the process, about Nita and Lance: "It was not like her to question his judgment." This time her loyalty is rewarded, and Lance, after Tetlow is jailed and charged with murder, his herds dispersed, and his gunmen killed off, rides off with her to his sequestered homestead. Cain Brockman is also in the cast of characters. He had been talked out of a confrontation with Kilkenny in "A Man Called Trent" and now the two are friends and allies. In a brief résumé of the previous Kilkenny stories—neither of which had appeared outside the pages of pulp magazines at the time KILKENNY was first published as an original paperback novel—the events in the Live

Oak country are recounted followed by those in "the cedar breaks of New Mexico where Kilkenny had been trying to establish a home." Even though the new Bantam edition of KILKENNY appeared five years *after* the reworked THE MOUNTAIN VALLEY WAR where the location had been changed to Idaho, L'Amour made no effort to alter this miniscule reference to the earlier story so as to be consistent. Also his counting was off here, as it is in LAST STAND AT PAPAGO WELLS (1957). A gunman starts out with three men accompanying him, only for two to be shot, and then walks "out on the street with his two remaining men."

"The Trail to Crazy Man" by Jim Mayo was published in *West* (7/48) and was later expanded into a paperback original by Louis L'Amour first published by Ace Books in 1954 as CROSSFIRE TRAIL. It belongs to the second major plot group: the hidden wealth story. The hero, Rafe Caradec, has been shanghaied and escapes from the ship after beating the skipper's "face into a gory pulp." The Ernest Haycox hero, as the Luke Short hero, is a man alone against all the odds. It was their serials that dominated the high-paying slick magazine markets in the late 1930s and 1940s—*Collier's* and *The Saturday Evening Post*. Going against this trend in his pulp stories, it is never so for the L'Amour hero. Even if at the beginning of the story the hero is alone, rapidly along the way he picks up sympathizers who join him in his battle. In Rafe Caradec's case, Tex Brisco, one of the men who escapes with him, decides to side him in his effort to ride to Painted Rock, a town in Wyoming, where he intends to save the ranch belonging to Charles

Rodney, a man they befriended aboard ship but who has died as a result of a number of beatings administered by the skipper. Obviously L'Amour was influenced somewhat in this story by Zane Grey's THE BORDER LEGION (1916) since the two principal villains who want possession of the Rodney ranch because of the oil to be found on it, Bruce Barkow and Dan Shute, bear more than a little resemblance to Kells and Gulden in Grey's novel. Rodney's wife has died in the interim and his daughter, the heroine Ann, is in love with Barkow, or at least she thinks she is until Rafe arrives on the scene. Rafe announces that "'I promised her father I'd take care of her, and I will, whether she likes it or not!'" Rafe goes up against Trigger Boyne, a gun slick in the employ of Barkow and Shute, and he walks so swiftly toward him that Boyne is rattled. Rafe guns him and, right after, turns and shoots another killer hidden in an upper story room. Rafe is brought to trial and Barkow figures it will be Rafe Caradec's finish since the judge is on his side. In a bit of gratuitous history, a characteristic that would become increasingly commonplace in L'Amour's fiction, Rafe asks that Ann be empanelled on the jury and reminds the judge that "'women served on juries in Laramie in eighteen seventy, and one was servin' as justice of the peace that year.'"

"Showdown Trail" by Jim Mayo was published in *Giant Western* (Winter, 48) and was expanded to form the novel, THE TALL STRANGER, published as a paperback original by Fawcett Gold Medal in 1957 and was adapted for the screen that same year as THE TALL STRANGER (Allied Artists, 1957), quite a good Western starring Joel McCrea and Virginia Mayo. Rock Bannon is the hero and the story is a variety of L'Amour's waylaid wagon train plot. Bannon had been found on the trail with two bullet wounds and was nursed back to health by the heroine, Sharon Crockett, who with her father is among a group of settlers who have formed a wagon train to get to California. The villain is Morton Harper who convinces the people in the wagon train to take a shortcut, despite Bannon's counsel against it, and, once he leads them to Indian Writing, he persuades most of the settlers to remain right there and homestead. The area the settlers choose for their town site is on Hardy Bishop's range. Bishop adopted Rock Bannon as his son after Rock's parents were killed by Kaw Indians, and Rock tries his best to maintain the peace. In this he fails because it is Harper's plan to get the settlers and Bishop's riders to kill off each other so he can have the valley for himself. Ultimately Bannon succeeds in upsetting Harper's scheme and Harper attempts a getaway, kidnapping Sharon in the process. Bannon trails them. One of L'Amour's strongest attributes as a Western writer could be exercised in a situation where he was describing a man on the trail replete with appropriate kaleidoscopic details: "The country grew rougher, but he shifted from draw to draw, cut across a flat, barren plateau of scattered rocks and rabbit grass, traversed a lava flow, black and ugly, to skirt a towering rust red cliff. A notch in the cliff ahead seemed to indicate a point of entry, so he guided the stallion among the boulders. A lizard darted from under the stallion's hoofs, and overhead a buzzard wheeled in wide, lonely circles." When Bannon catches up with the fugitive, Harper gets the drop on him. Rock resorts to the cigarette trick. He rolls a cigarette and then lights a match, all the time talking with Harper. He lets the match burn down to his fingers, distracting Harper's attention just long enough for him to reach for his gun and shoot. It would not be the last time in L'Amour's fiction that a hero would use the cigarette trick to get out of a tight spot. Bannon tells Sharon of Harper: "'At the wrong time he was too filled with hate to even accomplish a satisfactory killin'.'"

"The Rider of the Ruby Hills" by Jim Mayo appeared in *West* (9/49) and was not expanded to an original paperback novel until it appeared as WHERE THE LONG GRASS BLOWS, published by Bantam in 1976. In its original pulp version it served as the basis for the film, TREASURE OF RUBY HILLS (Allied Artists, 1955), starring Zachary Scott and Carole Mathews. The story employs L'Amour's basic range war plot. The hero is Ross Haney who is twenty-seven, broke, but armed with two six-guns and a Winchester. He rides into the district and feels that "it was a good country, a country where a man could live and grow, and where if he was lucky, he might have sons to grow tall and straight beside him." The two big ranches are the RR—owned by Chalk Reynolds—and the Box N—owned by Walt Pogue. There is a persistent rivalry between them, actually instigated by the master villain, Star Levitt, who is using the occasion to rustle from both men and who intends to see that they kill each other off so he can claim their spreads. "'There's an old law, Río,'" Ross Haney tells his horse, "'that only the strong survive. . . . Those ranches belong to men who were strong, and some of them still are. They were strong enough to take them from other men, from smaller men, weaker men.'" Ross is alone when he arrives but soon he has managed to gather a number of allies in his cause.

"The Trail to Peach Meadow Canyon" by Jim Mayo was published in *Giant Western* (10/49) and was substantially expanded to form SON OF A WANTED MAN published as an original paperback by Bantam in 1984. What L'Amour did in the expansion was to add episodes, only peripherally related to the original plot, featuring Borden Chantry and Tyrel Sackett who first meet in the 1978 Bantam paperback novel, BORDEN CHANTRY. Tyrel Sackett was introduced in THE DAYBREAKERS (1960), a novel set in the years following the Civil War. Tell Sackett, the eldest of the brothers, is off in Dakota Territory fighting Indians; Tyrel, his older brother Orrin, their younger brothers Bob and Joe, and their pipe-smoking mother all want to head West from their home in Tennessee. This novel is narrated in the first person by Tyrel, permitting L'Amour to employ his loosely episodic mode of plotting that he used regularly in the Sackett saga and in which what keeps the story moving is a constant series of emergencies, dangers, and plot complications, none of which is necessarily related to the central plot. In commenting on his pulp stories, L'Amour observed that "the essentials demanded by our editors were action and color, but, above all, one had to tell a story with a beginning, a middle, and an end. And the story had to move." The way in which L'Amour assured that all of his stories moved was precisely to introduce a new plot complication every thousand words or so. What is somewhat different in the Sackett books is that these plot complications can often take a reader rather far afield from the main story, bound to the central plot only by the device of the first person narrator and the focus on his various experiences. THE DAYBREAKERS for its central plot employs a variation of the range war plot: Jonathan Pritts has organized a gang of renegades and proceeds to New Mexico, intent on taking *Don* Luis Alvardo's Spanish land grant away from him and keeping it for himself. In this he is foiled ultimately by Tyrel Sackett who has fallen in love with *Don* Luis's daughter Drusilla. At one point when Tyrel is surrounded by Pritts's renegades, one of them holding a rifle on him, Tyrel uses the cigarette trick although he does not normally smoke, the match burning down to his fingers a sufficient distraction to allow him to draw his gun and do some fast shooting. In one of the longer subplots Tyrel rides off with another character to prospect for gold in Montana. Once at the mining camp, Tyrel becomes aware of the fact that Martin Brady, the local saloon owner, and his two henchmen have been preying upon the prospectors, taking their gold through gambling and whiskey and ambushing them if they try to leave the district with their gold. Sackett confronts Brady in a showdown and in strident L'Amour rhetoric informs him of what the score is: " 'Brady, this country is growing up. Folks are moving in and they want schools, churches, and quiet towns where they can walk in the streets of an evening.' . . . Right then I felt sorry for Martin Brady, although his kind would outlast my kind because people have a greater tolerance for evil than for violence. If crooked gambling, thieving, and robbing are covered over, folks will tolerate it longer than outright violence, even when the violence may be cleansing." All in all, about three years elapse before Tyrel finally manages to run off Pritts and settle down with Drusilla on the land grant. In the interim, Ma and the rest of the family have come West to New Mexico and, although New Mexico would not achieve statehood until 1912, Tyrel remarks that "already they were talking about Orrin for the United States Senate. . . ."

Some of L'Amour's early pulp stories were detective fiction, later reprinted in THE HILLS OF HOMICIDE (1983). BORDEN CHANTRY is a Western with a detective story plot. Joe Sackett, now grown to manhood, arrives in the nameless town where Chantry is the town marshal. He is murdered and the story is the narrative of Chantry's successful investigation, tracking a serial murderer in which Joe Sackett's murder is only the latest depredation. Unfortunately a detective story requires extremely careful plotting, too painstaking and detailed to be well suited to the one draft, no rewrite approach L'Amour took in writing his Bantam books, and all manner of ridiculous inconsistencies emerge. The focus is constantly on Chantry, so the reader is dismayed when Chantry discovers a .52-caliber rifle used by the murderer only for it to drop from sight without explanation when Chantry crosses the street to the hotel, as is also the case when Chantry, during the denouement, suddenly relates how he investigated the death of the previous marshal and recalls a talk he had with the local doctor although, in the time frame the reader is given, there would have been no opportunity for him to have done it.

"The Trail to Peach Mountain Canyon" is actually the shortest of the seven pulp short novels that L'Amour later expanded, and, therefore, was most in need of additional subplots and padding. Although he was willing to admit privately his concern about claims concerning copyright infringement from the magazine owners, publicly L'Amour insisted that "pleased as I was about how I brought the characters and their adventures to life in the pages of magazines, I still wanted the reader to know more about my people and why they did what they did." In "The Trail to Peach Meadow Canyon", young Mike Bastian is the adopted son of outlaw leader Ben Curry. As such, this is a variety of the initiation into manhood plot. Mike has been raised, ever since he was orphaned, to take over Ben's criminal operations once Ben decides to retire. His big choice is whether to become a criminal or not. In the course of the story, Mike learns that Ben has long been secretly married and has two daughters, the younger of whom Mike meets and the two fall in love at first sight. Her name is Drusilla. There is a mutiny in Ben's gang, several of the toughs wanting to take it over themselves. Mike finds himself in the company of Drusilla on the trail of an outlaw named Ducrow who has kidnapped Ben's older daughter Julie. Mike and Ducrow shoot it out in sequestered Peach Meadow Canyon after which they return to Ben's hideout only to learn that he and his loyal followers have stood off the mutiny and now Ben can retire with his swag. Mike and Drusilla decide to take up cattle ranching in Peach Meadow Canyon.

In expanding this short novel into SON OF A WANTED MAN, L'Amour commented: "I was able to follow in more detail what happened to the various groups of outlaws operating out of their canyon hideout and bringing them into contact with two law officers of the time and area, Tyrel Sackett and Borden Chantry, neither of whom is aware they are distantly related." *That* story L'Amour intended to narrate elsewhere. What his additions in the expansion came down to were that a splinter group of outlaws breaks off from the Ben Curry gang and intends to rob the bank in the still nameless town where Borden Chantry has now become sheriff.

"Showdown on the Hogback" by Jim Mayo was published in *Giant Western* (8/50). This short novel was expanded into an original paperback titled SHOWDOWN AT YELLOW BUTTE, published by Ace in 1953. The story is basically a variation of the range war plot. In SHOWDOWN AT YELLOW BUTTE the town is called Mustang and the normal situation is "a killing every day. . . ." The hero is Captain Tom Kedrick. He has been sent for by a friend, John Gunter, who is in a partnership with Alton Burwick and Colonel Loren Keith. The heroine is Consuelo Duane, Gunter's niece, who has lent her uncle the money to buy into Burwick's scheme. Keith is merely a tool of Burwick's. Burwick has laid claim to the ranches and farms in the district and he wants Kedrick to lead his men against these squatters and drive them out within ten days. Kedrick, as Lance Kilkenny in similar circumstances, soon realizes "it was a fight between a bunch of hard-working men against the company, made up largely of outsiders, seeking to profit from the work of local people." Kedrick switches sides and successfully leads the local people against Burwick's renegades. It turns out—absurdly—that in the past Burwick was a white renegade who led an Indian attack on a wagon train while wearing a suit of armor that so impressed the Indians that they followed him. Added to the range war plot is the plot of hidden wealth—it appears that a gold shipment that Burwick was after had been buried somewhere in the district and for this reason he wanted all of the local people forced off their land.

It is evident in any objective critical survey that L'Amour's magazine fiction in most cases is far superior to his later original paperback fiction for Bantam Books, despite the fact that the later books accounted for his increasing wealth, fame, and tremendous sales figures. The reason for this, I suspect, is that magazine editors were more demanding than were L'Amour's later editors at Bantam. Leo Margulies, the general editor at Standard Magazines where much of L'Amour's early pulp fiction was published, had a close personal working relationship with L'Amour, and he was very punctilious in matters of consistency and plausibility. L'Amour's idea of writing only a first draft and refusing to revise it really came about in the Bantam years. When he was a magazine writer, L'Amour would often write a second and even a third draft prior to submission in order to attain a level of acceptable literary quality. After L'Amour's death, his son, Beau L'Amour, discovered a box of earlier drafts of his father's pulp stories, and, although inferior to the finished stories that had already been published, Bantam began issuing these early drafts in new hard cover L'Amour story collections. Irwyn Applebaum, L'Amour's last editor at Bantam prior to L'Amour's death, confided to me that no one at Bantam would even read a L'Amour manuscript before it was placed into production. L'Amour's popularity was such and the author himself was so fundamentally opposed to editorial intervention of any kind that no one dared to interfere.

"Riders of the Dawn" by Louis L'Amour was published in *Giant Western* (6/51). It was later expanded to form SILVER CANYON, published in a hard cover edition by Avalon Books in 1956 with a $250 advance for the author; there were no royalties. Of course, L'Amour had been better paid by the pulp magazine, but he wanted to have a book of his published in a hard cover edition. The story is narrated in the first person by Matt Sabre—the Mathurin Sabre who appears in such short stories as "Ride, You Tonto Riders!" in *New Western Magazine* (8/49) and "The Marshal of Painted Rock" in *Triple Western Magazine* (2/53), the latter appearing two years after "Riders of the Dawn" in a different pulp magazine also published by Standard Magazines. Matt's name in the pulp short novel is spelled Mathieu Sabre and it is said that he is a gunfighter and former lawman. Matt rides into Hattan's Point and discovers that the district is in the midst of a range war. Rud Maclaren of the Bar M and Jim Pinder of the CP outfit both want the water located on the Two Bar, a ranch owned by a man named Ball. The heroine is Olga Maclaren, Rud's daughter, and Matt falls in love with her at first sight. Morgan Park is the master villain and secretly behind all the trouble. He has discovered silver on Maclaren's land and hopes Maclaren and Pinder will kill off each other so he can lay claim to the Bar M. Matt joins forces with Ball and is soon aided by the Benaras, six deadly gunfighters—another early rehearsal of the Sacketts. Matt comments: " 'The murderers, cheats, and swindlers must be stamped out before the honest citizens can have peace.' " Matt hires a man to teach him how to box so that, when he goes up against Morgan Park, he is able to win the fight. By the end, Park is killed by an Indian and the crooked lawyer working with him is exposed by Matt in a trial scene similar to that which concludes "The Trail to Crazy Man".

L'Amour first tried to write a true book-length Western novel with WESTWARD THE TIDE. No American publisher was willing to publish it, so L'Amour finally sold it to a British paperback publisher, World's Work, whose standard offer was £75 for British Empire rights in perpetuity. There had been since 1790 a provision in the Copyright Act of the United States known as *ad interim*. From the beginning until it was abandoned with the revised Copyright Act of 1978, this provision required an

American author who caused a book to be published by a publisher outside the United States to arrange for publication by an American publisher within a five-year period following first foreign publication or the work would fall into the Public Domain in the United States. That is what happened to WESTWARD THE TIDE, which wasn't published in the United States until it was issued with an unaltered text by Bantam Books in 1977. This novel utilizes the waylaid wagon train plot. The hero is gunfighter Matt Bardoul. He meets the heroine, Jacquine Coyle, on the stage to Deadwood and is so attracted to her that he decides to join in the venture supposedly headed up by her father Brian Coyle and a man calling himself Clive Massey, who turns out to be a notorious Civil War renegade leader by the name of Sim Boyne. The most interesting aspect of L'Amour's first paperback novel is that its ideology is so totally at odds with what he came later to believe and that he did not bother to excise from the text when the book was reprinted almost three decades later. First, there is the conservation theme. "In the short view," L'Amour wrote, "there was much good in the westward trek, but in the long view it was a mad rush of greed and rapine, the lust of men who ripped the wealth from the land and then deserted it. . . . Like a young man who inherits a fortune the people of the country were spending their birthright in a wild orgy of finance and greed, heedless of the years to come." L'Amour was even more outspoken in his defense of the Indians "'The white man came and the beaver are gone, the buffalo are going,'" Matt remarks. "'The white man cuts the timber along the streams and causes floods that formerly the roots and brush held back. Already, in some places, he is putting too much stock on the grass, overgrazing the country.'" In contrast to the white men are the Indians. "'In all recorded history,'" Matt continues, "'there is no more tragic epitaph to a beaten, dying people who have been robbed of their birthright than that uttered by Spotted Tail when he said, "'The land is full of white men; our game is all gone, and we have come upon great trouble.'"

A wagon train of well-to-do settlers and their families is being organized by Coyle and Massey, headed to the Big Horns where ostensibly gold has been discovered, and these settlers can both mine gold and build a town. Each family has to buy into the venture and pack into wagons all that will be needed to found such a town once they arrive. Massey's ultimate intention is to seize the wagon train, once it is safe to do so, kill off those who resist, enslave the others to build him a town, then kill them, giving the women to his renegades as a reward. Accordingly Massey does not want Matt along. He hires a professional gunfighter to go up against Matt before they pull out, but Matt walks so fast in the gunfighter's direction that he is unnerved and humiliated and finally forced to leave town. It is a ploy that became increasingly commonplace. On the trail Matt beats up one of Massey's riders, explaining that he is so good with his fists because—as Lance Kilkenny and others before him—he has studied boxing, and also, as Leo Margulies told his editors, fight scenes are so important to any story that they must never be cut.

Matt is a believer in violence. "'There are Indians here,'" he tells Jacquine, "'and white renegades that are worse. These men are savage, they understand only the law of force, and if one is to live in such a country one must be prepared to protect those one loves and the things one lives by.'" Matt is a self-educated gunfighter, quoting Schopenhauer and explaining that "'around these campfires I've heard men discuss questions of philosophy in a manner that would do justice to Berkeley and Hume.'" However, because L'Amour wrote this book rapidly, there are serious errors in construction. The renegades steal all the ammunition from the settlers' wagons. Matt reflects on their situation and comes to realize that "as things stood, in a prolonged battle, all the advantage lay with the renegades due to their stealing of ammunition." Yet, four pages later, it turns out that Matt has known nothing about the ammunition having been stolen!

That same year "Guns of the Timberlands" by Jim Mayo appeared in *West* (9/50). The hero is Clay Bell who runs his cattle on Deep Creek range. The trees on that range provide a needed watershed. However, Jud Devitt and his loggers come to town with the intention of harvesting the Deep Creek timber. Sam Tinker, who founded the town, tells heroine Colleen Riley that there are two kinds of men: "'Them that come to build and them come to get rich and get out.'" In L'Amour's West, it is always the builders—in contrast to history—who are the big winners, and this case is no exception. The master villain responsible for importing Jud Levitt and his loggers is the local banker, Noble

Wheeler, a man who, "knowing the way of war . . . realized both sides would lose in the end. And that, he decided as he rubbed fat hands together, was exactly as he wanted it." Subsequently L'Amour expanded this pulp novel into a hardcover Western published as GUNS OF THE TIMBERLANDS by Jason Press in 1955. It was adapted for the screen as GUNS OF THE TIMBERLANDS (Warner, 1960), starring Alan Ladd and Jeanne Crain. The story employs the basic range war plot of KILKENNY and other early L'Amour stories, only instead of cattle being moved onto the local range from the outside the invasion is that of Jud Levitt and his loggers.

The 1950s would be a very good decade for L'Amour, with no less than nine Western films based on his fiction. Although there had been a problem finding a publisher for WESTWARD THE TIDE, Leo Margulies came to L'Amour with a most attractive proposal that could lead to an entire series of hardcover books. Standard Magazines had negotiated a deal with Doubleday where the magazine publisher would launch a new pulp titled *Hopalong Cassidy's Western Magazine*. Each issue would feature a novel about Hopalong Cassidy written under a house name, Tex Burns, stories that L'Amour would be paid to write. Doubleday would then publish these novels in hardcover editions. A conflict, however, emerged almost at once. Doubleday wanted the stories to feature a sanitized image of Hopalong. Instead of the red-headed, hard-drinking, cigarette-, cigar-, and pipe-smoking roustabout Clarence E. Mulford had created, a man who began working for the Bar-20 when barely out of his teens and who aged until he was in his sixties in the last of Mulford's novels, HOPALONG CASSIDY SERVES A WRIT (1941), the Hopalong in the new books was to be based on the image of William Boyd in the theatrical films that were now so successfully playing on television. For the first story, "Rustlers of West Fork" by Tex Burns in *Hopalong Cassidy's Western Magazine* (Fall, 50), L'Amour, who had studied Mulford's books, gave the readers Mulford's character. This was totally unacceptable to Doubleday, so L'Amour was asked to rewrite the story before Doubleday would publish it. Hopalong came out looking this way: "Clad entirely in black, from his sombrero to his ebony-hued boots, he was a striking figure—a man to attract attention anywhere. In marked contrast to his dark range clothes were his white hair, his silver spurs, and the two white bone-handled silver six-guns. . . ." In L'Amour's Tex Burns stories, this figure, clad in what Harry Sherman, the original producer of the Hopalong Cassidy theatrical films, had once called Boyd's "monkey suit", moves among ranchers and thieves without anyone laughing at his outlandish costume. His favorite horse is the white stallion, Topper. This Hoppy neither smokes nor drinks although he does chew gum. He has cold blue eyes and, despite the white hair, is said to be a young man.

The commission had come about because Clarence E. Mulford did not want to write any more Hopalong Cassidy stories. L'Amour, because he had studied the Mulford books, included some of Mulford's series characters in these new stories:

Red Connors, Tex Ewalt, and Mesquite Jenkins. L'Amour almost paraphrased Mulford in describing the Bar-20 spirit, but with an element of his own that he would employ in the Sackett saga, a series certainly inspired by Mulford's long Bar-20 saga. In BAR-20 DAYS (1911), Mulford observed that it was "the quality of friendship which bound the units of the Bar-20 outfit into a smooth firm whole. They were like brothers, like one man." For L'Amour, the Bar-20 "had worked as a team for so long that they could easily guess what the others were doing at any given time." Mulford's Hopalong was a man of violence. There is a scene in BAR-20 (1907) in which it said of Hopalong that "never in all his life had he felt such a desire to kill. His eyes were diamond points of accumulated fury, and those whom he faced quailed before him." L'Amour, the man who had created Kilkenny and numerous other pulp heroes who were not afraid to use lethally guns or fists when necessary, now had to restrain himself to make credible a Hopalong who had a reputation for avoiding violence and gunplay whenever possible. This Hopalong would shoot a villain's gun out of his hand, rather than plug him. He tries only to wound a villain when in a gun battle, whereas Mulford's Hopalong Cassidy in the course of the saga would fatally discharge Judge Colt's justice at 200 men. The Hopalong in the Tex Burns stories, when an outlaw suffers a broken leg in a skirmish, sees to it that the man receives care and attention. When attacked by a villain during a stampede, Hopalong knocks him unconscious in order to drag him to safety. When it comes time for the big cleanup, this Hopalong has to remark: "'Let's hope we can do it without killing.'" In a final showdown with master villains, however, Hopalong is not above shooting them down in a fair gunfight.

"Rustlers of West Fork" from the first issue of *Hopalong Cassidy's Western Magazine* is something of a collector's item because it is the only L'Amour Hopalong Cassidy story to be published featuring Mulford's character. The book version, HOPALONG CASSIDY AND THE RUSTLERS OF WEST FORK (1951), was successfully sanitized to project the desired image. To make matters worse, the new magazine proved a disappointment on newsstands and ended with the second issue, *Hopalong Cassidy's Western Magazine* (Winter, 51), featuring a sanitized "Trail to Seven Pines" by Tex Burns. The four Tex Burns books were scrupulously edited, and sometimes even partially rewritten through editorial intervention at Doubleday. L'Amour, who was paid a flat fee of $500 a book as work for hire, detested what had happened. When I sent him his bibliography as it had been prepared for the ENCYCLOPEDIA OF FRONTIER AND WESTERN FICTION, L'Amour objected to these books being included among his works. "The situation was this," he wrote to me, "during a period after the collapse of the magazine field when all the pulps and many other publications went under, I was asked to write four Hopalong Cassidy novels. This was during the sudden boom that followed his popularity on TV. I assured the publisher that the books would not sell. The fans of Hopalong were kids and they could get all they wanted in comic books about Hopalong. Moreover, I viewed the Boyd Hopalong with some distaste. However, they preferred to believe that the books would sell and I was paid a flat fee to write them. . . . Being broke I was in no position to argue. I wrote the books and they supported me during a very bad year." When I responded that nothing in what he had said indicated that he had not written these books and, therefore, they belonged in his bibliography, L'Amour became even more adamant: "To attribute those books to me, in any sense, would not be a credit to your accuracy. The best thing I can advise, in all sincerity and goodwill, is to forget my connection with them. I deserve no more credit than would a President's speechwriter . . . and I have never yet seen one of them given credit. I am trying to help you keep your book honest. If you intend to list those works as mine I shall insist you also list every essay my children have written with which I helped them as well as every other document I can scrape up in which I had a hand. It would make just as much sense."

There is in these Hopalong Cassidy books the inimitable L'Amour rhetoric: " 'We need homes, schools, churches here, and we can have them, but before we can have peace, we must be rid of those men who cling to the old way of doing things.' " I was willing to concede that L'Amour did have a point—that the interpolations of descriptions of the William Boyd image into his Tex Burns stories were definitely a betrayal of his original intentions in writing the stories, but he was nonetheless their author. The whole issue was settled posthumously when Bantam reprinted the Doubleday books under the Louis L'Amour byline as hardcovers with an afterword by Beau L'Amour admitting that his father had written them. In the end it is unfortunate that, since at last the books were being published under his name, Louis L'Amour's original versions could not have been used, rather than the bowdlerized Doubleday texts.

L'Amour's big break, the one that put him firmly on the road to success, came the same year Doubleday published the last of Tex Burns's titles. "The Gift of Cochise" by Louis L'Amour was published in *Collier's* (7/5/52). It marked the first time a L'Amour story had appeared in a slick magazine. In this story, Angie Lowe lives in Apache country with her seven-year-old son Jimmy and her five-year-old daughter Jane. Her husband, Ed Lowe, has gone to El Paso for supplies and he dallies there, drinking and gambling. He is not a bad man, simply an irresponsible one. Cochise comes to visit Angie in Ed's absence and is impressed by her spirit and the spirit of her son. He will allow Angie to wait, unmolested, for the return of her man. In a barroom brawl in El Paso, Ed Lowe steps into a gunfight between hero Ches Lane and the three Tolliver brothers, getting killed in the fracas. Ches learns that Lowe had a wife and two children and heads out to pay them his respects and to see if he can be of some help. On the way there, he is surrounded by Apaches and defeats one of the warriors in a knife fight. This wins him the admiration of Cochise. When Lane finds Angie, the Apaches regard him as her man, a feeling she comes to share.

"The Gift of Cochise" was purchased for John

Wayne's Batjac Productions by Wayne and Robert Fellows who wanted to produce it for the screen. James Edward Grant, Wayne's favorite screenwriter, did the screenplay, with Warner Bros. financing and releasing the film. Grant changed the original plot considerably, beginning with the character of the hero, now called Hondo Lane. In HONDO (Warner, 1953) Hondo was given a dog named Sam as a companion. John Ford acted as an unofficial adviser on the picture, wanting to do what he could to make Wayne's venture into film production a success. L'Amour had not, as yet, been able to interest any American book publisher in his fiction, other than for the Tex Burns books, which were not his idea. He got Batjac to agree to let him novelize James Edward Grant's screenplay and publish it under his own name, as if it were totally *his* story, and he even got Wayne to allow himself to be quoted that HONDO, published by Fawcett Gold Medal in 1953 to coincide with release of the film, was the finest Western he had ever read. Subsequently L'Amour always claimed that HONDO—when not even the title had been his—was his first novel rather than WESTWARD THE TIDE. Nor would this be the last time that L'Amour would novelize a screenplay and publish it under his own name. He would again in HOW THE WEST WAS WON (1963), based on James R. Webb's Academy Award-winning original story and screenplay. There is no particular dishonor when a writer engages in hack work for the purpose of making money. Lewis B. Patten, for example, wrote two books in the Gene Autry book series about Autry's adventures that were supposedly written by Autry himself, but he felt no qualms about including these titles in his bibliography. L'Amour, on the other hand, because he was creating as much a legend about himself as he was writing Western fiction was willing to take credit for HONDO but not for the Tex Burns books. Quixotically L'Amour did not renew the original story, "The Gift of Cochise", when he was supposed to in the twenty-eighth year, and so now that story, too, is in the Public Domain.

L'Amour's novelization of HONDO follows Grant's screenplay very closely, using much of Grant's dialogue. Angie Lowe was retained as the heroine, but the daughter Jane was abandoned. Angie has only her young son Johnny. Her husband is a wicked man and he has deserted her. Hondo, together with his dog Sam, arrives at the Lowe ranch and stays around to help out. Later, in a fight in the desert, Hondo kills Lowe when Lowe tries to steal his horse. L'Amour did add one scene to the novel not in the screenplay, a sexual episode between Hondo and Angie before Hondo tells her that he has killed her husband. Cochise was changed to Vittoro. Another of L'Amour's contributions to the novelization was to incorporate his view of marriage when he reflected about Angie and Hondo that "this was as it should be . . . a man and a woman working toward something, for something. Not apart, but a team." L'Amour also accepted Grant's view of the Indian wars, and henceforth this would remain his posture, as opposed to the view he espoused in WESTWARD THE TIDE. The Apaches "saw the white men endlessly coming, their many soldiers, their many ponies, their food supply that was endless, and their many cartridges of brass. The Apache knew his hour was past. He knew the white men would take even this last land, but it was not in him to buckle under. He would fight, sing his death song, and die."

Three years after HONDO, considering himself financially secure at last, L'Amour married Katherine Elizabeth Adams, and from this union came their two children, son Beau and daughter Angelique. In the meantime, on the basis of the success of HONDO as a film—more than a decade later it would inspire a short-lived television series—L'Amour began vigorously to market his stories to motion picture producers. He expanded five of his pulp novels to form paperback Westerns in the 1950s and wrote nine additional original paperback titles. If I have seemed critical of L'Amour's expansions of his pulp novels, this is certainly not intended to single him out. Many Western writers did this in the face of the expanding original paperback Western market and the shrinking pulp magazine market. Rarely are any of these expansions particularly successful, in part because the authors felt they had to make the stories sufficiently different so as to avoid a charge of copyright infringement and because the stories had to be expanded to greater length in order to accommodate the paperback publishers. This almost invariably destroyed the stories as originally conceived and neither the characters nor the situations could withstand such an expansion without much of the quality of the original story being compromised. It has been my experience that a story frequently has an ideal length, and much of the effectiveness and drama of it is intrinsically bound up with the length the author chose in which to tell it in the first place. L'Amour's short novels, written originally for magazines like *Giant Western* and *West*, will of necessity always be best in the form in which they first appeared.

L'Amour did not entirely abandon his Jim Mayo pseudonym once he turned almost exclusively to writing paperback Western novels. UTAH BLAINE by Jim Mayo was published in 1954 by Ace Books, and it was filmed under this title by Columbia Pictures in 1957. KILKENNY was filmed as BLACK-JACK KETCHUM, DESPERADO (Columbia, 1956) the year L'Amour married. In this transition to paperback Westerns L'Amour had his basic plots, forged in the days he wrote for pulp magazines, and he found no reason to alter what continued to work for him. UTAH BLAINE uses the range war plot. The two biggest ranches in the district are owned by men who built them up from nothing, and, as the story opens, they are coveted by greedy men who came later and found the best land already taken. Blaine interposes himself into this conflict and it becomes personal when one of the big ranches is left to him, which is just about what happens to Matt Sabre in SILVER CANYON. In FLINT (1960), the eponymous hero believes he is dying of cancer, and, after having been a success during his years in the East, he returns to the West in order to die. What he encounters is the range war plot. Similar to Ross Haney in "The Rider of the Ruby Hills", Flint knows about a hideout in the badlands where, in this case, wild horses are trapped. As happens to Jim Gatlin in the short story, "The Black Rock Coffin Makers" in *.44 Western* (2/50), Flint scales a sharp V in a canyon wall to escape from a tight spot.

With the publication of RADIGAN (1958), Bantam Books became L'Amour's exclusive paperback publisher. It was a stroke of extremely good fortune. Frederick G. Glidden was under contract to Bantam to receive a $15,000 advance for every original Luke Short novel he would write, but instead of submitting two books a year as called for by the contract, over the previous decade he had only sent in eight. Saul David, a Bantam editor, asked L'Amour if he could write two new books each and every year. L'Amour said he could. As the years passed, Bantam came up with the marketing strategy of keeping *all* L'Amour titles in print, and, as his number of paperback novels progressed, this meant that very often in Western paperback racks at least half the available titles were books by Louis L'Amour. This strategy was the same, in its way, as Jared Tetlow's scheme of overrunning the available range with his cattle herds and it proved effective to an astonishing degree. L'Amour also decided to merchandise himself. Western writers, with perhaps the exception of Zane Grey, have always tended to be rather retiring. It was not so with L'Amour. He dressed up in fancy cowboy outfits, traveled about the United States in a motor home, making personal appearances and promoting himself at every available opportunity. "Bantam did nothing for me," he once told me. "I did everything myself." Other than for their marketing strategy, I think this was the truth.

By the end of the 1970s, L'Amour grew restless. He wanted to write longer, more historical novels, and he wanted them to be published first in hardcover editions. It is to L'Amour's credit that he did try, when he was nearly seventy years old, to take a new direction in his Western fiction. Unfortunately, however, he refused to alter what now had become his method of composition since he had left the magazine markets—a first draft only without any revisions. The Saturday Review Press brought out hardbound editions of THE CALIFORNIOS (1974), SACKETT'S LAND (1974), OVER ON THE DRY SIDE (1975), and RIVERS WEST (1975), but the stories were so poorly constructed that reviews were devastating, and the publishing company was short-lived. E.P. Dutton took over the hardcover editions, publishing TO THE FAR BLUE MOUNTAINS in 1976 and BENDIGO SHAFTER in 1979. L'Amour was not pleased with the sales for TO THE FAR BLUE MOUNTAINS and, initially for BENDIGO SHAFTER, he submitted the book to Doubleday, the firm that had long ago published the Tex Burns books. Harold Kuebler, an editor at Doubleday, informed L'Amour that they would be willing to take on the book, provided L'Amour was willing to revise the manuscript in accordance with what was felt to be acceptable guidelines for trade fiction. This L'Amour refused to do. His books must be published exactly as he wrote them without any changes whatsoever.

In BENDIGO SHAFTER L'Amour used the first-person narrative he had pioneered in some of his early pulp short stories and in early paperback novels such as TO TAME A LAND (1956) and that he tended to prefer in writing his Sackett saga. L'Amour needed a beginning for this novel and so he went back to what happened after the events narrated in what I consider to be his finest short story, "War Party", published in *The Saturday Evening Post* (6/13/59). In this story, Mrs. Miles has just buried her husband. The story is narrated by her thirteen-year-old son Bud. Mrs. Miles, together with Bud and six-year-old Jeanie, wants to continue with the wagon train on its trek. There is the familiar L'Amour rhetoric: "This was a big country needing big men and women to live in it, and there was no place for the frightened or the mean. The prairie and sky had a way of trimming folks down to size, or changing them to giants to whom nothing seemed impossible." The story ends as Mrs. Miles leads a small group of settlers away from the main wagon train to build their homes in an ideal valley.

In BENDIGO SHAFTER the only characters retained from the short story by name are John Sampson and a man named Webb. Mrs. Miles was changed to Ruth Macken and she has only one child, twelve-year-old Bud. Cain Shafter and his wife, his younger brother Bendigo, and their sister Lorna, along with the guide Ethan Sackett, a distant relation to the Sackett family, are among the pioneers who follow Mrs. Macken to settle in a valley somewhere in Wyoming. One of the charms of "War Party" is its strong heroine. BENDIGO SHAFTER is late L'Amour and his view of the rôle to be played by women had changed and so Mrs. Macken undergoes a reduction from what Mrs.

Miles had been. When Bendigo Shafter, the narrator, tells Ethan Sackett that he regards Mrs. Macken as the real leader among them, Ethan corrects him. "'Mrs. Macken is a thinking woman who knows her mind,'" he says, "'but you watch and listen, Bendigo. You'll see she starts things. She opens the ball but nothing moves unless Cain says so. . . . A woman needs a man, Bendigo, even a woman like Ruth Macken. No woman, however strong, should have to stand alone. Believe me, she's a stronger woman because Cain is there and she knows he's there.'" To his theme that only the truly strong survive, L'Amour by this point had added another arrow to his string, that of one-settlement culture: "The Indian, like the buffalo, would pass from the face of the land or become one with those who came, for they were all caught up with change, the inevitable change that comes to men and towns and nations. Men move across the face of the world like tides upon the sea, and when they have gone, others will come; and the weak would pass and the strong would live, for that was the way it was, and the way it would be." After 1960, perhaps because he knew that a good many young people read his Western fiction, L'Amour undertook to sanitize his heroes much in the way his Hopalong Cassidy had become sanitized. There was no consistency in this. When he reprinted one of his earlier stories, the heroes were still seen drinking and smoking, but the later heroes were such as would have pleased a Ladies' Aid society. L'Amour kept insisting that his protagonists were not heroes, but they were increasingly men like Bendigo Shafter who always do the "right" thing, who do not drink, smoke, or curse, and who, unlike earlier L'Amour heroes, do not even drop their "g"s.

Despite the many subplots, complications, and accidental action episodes, BENDIGO SHAFTER is divided into three major parts, the first describing the building of the settlement during the first winter, the second describing Bendigo's journey farther West to secure a herd of cattle for the settlement, and the third describing Bendigo's trip East to New York in pursuit of the heroine who he eventually marries in typical ranch romance fashion. Dutton was unwilling to do another L'Amour book after this one, so L'Amour was finally compelled to convince Bantam Books itself to issue hardcover editions of his "big" novels while continuing to publish his ordinary original paperbacks. Bantam did accede to his idea, and no matter in which form a new L'Amour book appeared, it sold extremely well. In the end, he was right in his response to me that he did not think his readers would care if there was a discrepancy about the number of people killed in an Indian attack in LAST STAND AT PAPGO WELLS. In THE HAUNTED MESA (1987), one of L'Amour's "big" Westerns, combining science fantasy with a contemporary Western setting, a pickup truck suddenly turns into a car a few pages later, and one character dies, only to die a second time because the author had forgotten, or had not re-read, what he had already written. It did not matter to his readers.

"I am not a prophet," he told me during that first meeting at his home, "but I would predict that I am the only Western author writing today who will still be read twenty years from now." That was twenty-five years ago. He was wrong in general, but not about himself. He does still continue to be read by millions of readers of Western stories. At the end of his life he was able, as few were able for many decades in the United States, to die at his home. A few hours before he expired he was still at work, reading over the page proofs of his autobiography.

At his best, L'Amour was a master of spectacular action and stories with a vivid, propulsive forward motion. Unfortunately for literary critics and literary historians, it is the reading public that chooses the authors whose fiction enjoys favor beyond their lifetimes. In this respect, Louis L'Amour's popularity continues, as it has for Zane Grey and Max Brand. None of them has ever been out of print. This means basically one thing. These authors have proved able to attract new readers in each succeeding generation; there is something, perhaps intangible, about their fiction that endures and, seemingly, is constantly renewable. For Louis L'Amour personally, as an author of Western stories, that is no small achievement.

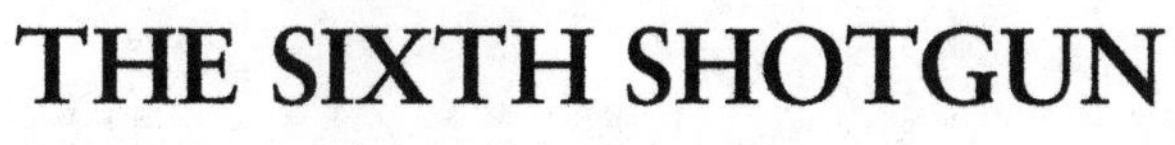

THE SIXTH SHOTGUN

They were hanging Leo Carver on Tuesday afternoon, and the loafers were watching the gallows go up. This was the first official hanging in the history of Cañon Gap, and the first gallows ever built in the territory. But then, the citizens at the Gap were always the kind to go in for style.

The boys from the ranches were coming in, and the hard-booted men from the mines, and the nine saloons were closing up, but only for the hour of the hanging. On the Street behind the Palace where the cottonwoods lined the creek, Fat Marie had given three hours off to the girls—one for the hanging and one for mourning and the third for drinking their tears away.

For Leo had been a spending man who would be missed along the street, and Leo had been a singing man with a voice as clear as a mountain echo and fresh as a long wind through the sage. And Leo was a handsome man, with a gun too quick to his hand. So they were hanging Leo Carver on the gallows in Cañon Gap, and the folks were coming in from the forks of every creek.

From behind the barred window Leo watched them working. "Build it high!!" he yelled at them. "And build it strong, for you're hanging the best man in Cañon Gap when tomorrow comes!"

Old Pap, who had prospected in the Broken Hills before the first foundation was laid at the Gap, took his pipe from his mouth and spat into the dust. "He's right at that," he said, "and no lie. If the 'Paches were coming over that hill right now, it's Leo Carver I'd rather have beside me than any man Jack in this town."

Editor Chafee nodded his head. "Nobody will deny that he's a fighting man," he agreed. "Leo was all right until civilization caught up with him."

And there it was said, a fit epitaph for him, if epitaph he'd have, and in their hearts not a man who heard it but agreed that what Chafee said was right.

"There'll be some," Old Pap added, "who'll feel a sigh of relief when they spring that trap. When Leo's neck is stretched and the sawbones says the dead word over him, many a man will stop sweating, you can bet on that."

"Better be careful what you say." Jase Ford shifted uneasily. "It ain't healthy to be hintin'."

"Not since they put Leo away, it ain't," Old Pap agreed, "but truth's a luxury the old can afford. There's nothing they can take from me but my life, and that's no use to me. And to do that they'd have to shoot me down from behind, and that's the sort of thing they'd do unless they could hang me legal, like Leo Carver's to be hung."

Nobody said anything, but Chafee looked gloomy as he stared at the gallows. There was no living doubt that Leo Carver was an outlaw. No doubt that he had rustled a few head here and there, no doubt that he had offended the nice people of the town by carousing at the Palace and down the Street of the cottonwoods. There was no doubt, either, that he'd stuck up the stage that night on the Rousensock—but from there on there was doubt aplenty.

Mitch Williams was dead, buried out there on boot hill with the others gone before him, Mitch Williams, the shotgun messenger who never lost a payload until that night on the Rousensock, the night that Leo Carver stuck up the stage. It was a strange story no matter how you looked at it, but Leo was a strange man, a strange man of dark moods and happy ones, but a man with a queer streak of gallantry in him, and something of a manner all his own.

Mitch had been up on the box that night when Leo Carver stepped from the brush. Oh, he was wearing a mask, all right, wearing a mask that covered his face. But who did not know it was Leo?

He stepped from the brush with a brace of six guns in his hands and said: "Hold those horses, Pete! You can. . . ." He broke off sharp there, for he saw Mitch.

Now Mitch Williams was a hand. He had that shotgun over his knees but the muzzle was away from Leo. Mitch could never have swung that shotgun around under Leo's gun, and he knew it. So did Doc Spender, who was stage driver. Leo Carver had that stage dead to rights and he had Mitch Williams helpless.

"Sorry, Mitch!" He said it loud and clear, so they all heard him. "I thought this was your night off. I'd never rob a stage you were on, and I'd never shoot you or force you to shoot me." He swung his horse. "So long!" And he was gone.

That was Leo for you. That was why they liked him along the Gila, and why as far away as the Nueces they told stories about him. But what happened after that was different.

The stage went on south. It went over the range through Six-Shooter Gap and there was another hold-up. There was a sudden blast of fire from the rocks and Mitch Williams toppled dead from the box, and then another blast—it was a shotgun—and Doc took a header into the brush and coughed out his life there in the mesquite.

Inside, they were sitting still and frightened. They heard somebody crawl up to the box and throw down the strongbox. They heard it hit, and then they heard somebody riding off. One horse, one rider.

The next morning they arrested Leo.

He was washing up at the time, and they'd waited for just that. He had his guns off and they took him without a fight. Not that he tried to make one. He didn't. He just looked surprised.

"Aw, fellers" he protested, "I never done nothing! What's the matter?"

"You call that nothing? You robbed the stage last night."

"Oh, that?" He just grinned. "Put down those guns, boys, I'll come along. Sure, you know by this time I didn't rob it. I just stuck it up for a lark, and, when I seen Mitch, I knowed it was no lark. That *hombre* would have sat still while I robbed it and drilled me when I left. He was a trusty man, that one."

"You said *was*, so I guess you know you killed him."

Leo's face changed then. "Killed who? Say, what is this?"

And then they told him, and his face turned gray and sick. He looked around at their faces and none of them was friendly. Mitch had been a family man, and so had Doc. Both of them well liked.

"I didn't do it," Leo said, "that was somebody else. I left 'em be."

"Until you could get a shotgun!" That was Mort Lewand, who shipped the money for the bank. "Like you said, Mitch would shoot. You knew that, and he had the gun on you, so you backed out. Then you came back later with a shotgun and shot him from ambush."

"That's not true." Leo was dead serious. "And he didn't have me covered. Mitch had that shotgun pointed the other way. I had the drop, and, if I'd been planning to kill him, I'd've shot him then."

Oh, they had a trial! Judge come over from Tucson to hold court. They had a trial and a big one. Folks came from all over, and they made a big thing of it. Not that there was much anybody could say for Leo.

Funny thing, that is. Most of us, right down inside, we knew the kind of man Leo Carver was, but most of what we knew wasn't evidence. Ever stop to think how hard it is to know a man isn't a murderer and yet know that your feeling he isn't ain't evidence?

They made it sound bad. Leo admitted he had killed seven men. Fair, stand-up fights, but still the men were dead by his gun. He admitted to rustling a few cows. Leo could have denied it, and maybe they couldn't have proved it in a court of law, but Leo wasn't used to the ways of courts and he knew darned well we all knew he had rustled them cows. Fact is, I don't think he ever thought of denying it.

He had stuck up a few stages, too. He admitted to that. But he denied killing Mitch Williams and he denied getting that strongbox. $20,000 it held. $20,000 in gold.

Everybody thought Webb Pascal would defend Leo, but he refused, said he wanted no part of it. Webb had played poker with Leo and they'd been friends, but Webb refused him. Leo took that mighty hard. Lane Moore refused him, too, so all he could do was get that drunken old Bob Keyes to handle his case.

Convicted? You know he was. That's why they are hanging him. Keyes couldn't defend a sick cat from a bath. When they got through asking questions of Leo Carver, he was a dead Injun, believe me.

He had tried to stick up the stage once. He was a known killer. He had rustled cows. He traveled with a bad element in Cañon Gap. He had no alibi. All he had, really, was his own statement that he hadn't done it—that and the thing we knew in our hearts that isn't admissible as evidence.

"Shame for you fellers to go to all that trouble," Leo said now. That was Leo. There was no stopping him. "Why don't we just call the whole thing off?"

Mort Lewand stood in his doorway, chewing his cigar and watching that gallows go up, and it made me sore, seeing it like that, for if ever a man had hated another, Mort Lewand had hated Leo.

Why? No particular reason. Personality, I'd guess you'd say. It was simply that they never tied up right. Mort, he pinched every dime he made. Leo spent his or gave it away. Mort went to church regular and was a rising young businessman. He was the town's banker and he owned the express company, and he had just bought one of the finest ranches in the country.

Leo never kept any money. He was a cattleman when he wanted to be, and as steady a hand as you'd find when he worked. One time he saved the CY herd almost single-handed when they got caught in a norther. He took on the job of ramrodding the Widow Ferguson's ranch after her old man was killed, and he tinkered and slaved and worked, doing the job of a half dozen hands until she had something she could sell for money enough to keep her.

Leo never kept a dime. He ate it up, drank it up, gave it away. The rest of the time he sat under the cottonwoods and played that old guitar of his and sang songs, old songs like my mother used to sing, old Scotch, Irish, and English songs, and some he made up as he went along.

He got into fights, too. He whipped the three Taylor boys single-handed one day. I remember that most particular because I was there. That was the day he got the blood on Ruth Hadlin's handkerchief.

The Hadlins were the town's society. Every town's got some society, and Judge Emory Hadlin was the big man of this town. He had money, all right, but he had name, too. Even in the West some folks set store by a name, and, whenever the judge said his name, it was like ringing a big gong. It had a sound. Maybe that was all some names had, but this one had more. Honor, reputation, square dealing, and no breath of scandal ever to touch any of them. Fine folks, and everybody knew it. Mort Lewand, he set his cap for Ruth but she never seemed to see him. That made him some angered, but tickled most of us. Mort figured he was mighty high-toned and it pleased us when Ruth turned him down flat.

Don't get the idea she was uppity. There was the time Old Pap came down with pneumonia. He was in a bad way and nobody to look after him but little Mary Ryan from down the street. Mary cared for him night and day almost until Ruth Hadlin heard about it.

She came down there and knocked on the door, and, when Mary opened it and saw Ruth, she turned seven colors. There she was, a mighty pert little girl, but she was from the Street, and here was Ruth Hadlin—well, they don't come any further apart.

Mary flushed and stammered and she didn't know what to say, but Ruth came right on in. She turned around and said: "How is he, Mary? I didn't even know he was ill."

Ill, that's what she said. We folks mostly said sick, instead of ill. Mary was shocked, too, never guessing that anybody like Ruth would know her name, or speak to her like that.

"He's bad off, Miss Ruth, but you shouldn't be here. This is the . . . it's the Street."

Ruth just looked at her and smiled, and she said: "I know it is, Mary, but Old Pap is ill and he can be just as ill on the Street as anywhere. I just heard about it, Mary, and how you've been caring for him. Now you go get some rest. I'll stay with him."

Mary hesitated, looking at that beautiful blue gown Ruth was wearing and at the shabby little cabin. "There ain't . . . isn't much to do," she protested.

"I know." Ruth was already bending over Old Pap and she just looked around and said: "By the way, Mary. Tell somebody to go tell Doctor Luther to come down here."

"We tried, Miss Ruth. He won't come. He said all his business was the other side of town, that he'd no time for down here."

She straightened up then. "You go tell him that Ruth Hadlin wants him down here!" Her voice was crisp. "He'll come."

He did, too.

But that was Miss Ruth. She was a thoroughbred, that one. And that was where she first met Leo Carver.

It was the third day she had been sharing and nursing with Mary Ryan, and she was in the shack alone when she heard that horse. He was coming hell-bent for election and she heard him pull up in front of the house, and then the door opened and in stepped Leo Carver.

She knew him right off. How could you miss him? He was two inches over six feet with shoulders wider than two of most men, and he was dark and clean-built with a fine line to his jaw, and he had cold gray eyes. He wore two guns and his range clothes, and right then he had a two-day growth of beard. It must have startled her. Here was a man known as an outlaw, a rustler, and a killer, and she was there alone with a sick man.

He burst in that door, and then drew up short, looking from Ruth to the sick old man. If he was surprised to find her there, he didn't let on. He just swept off his hat and asked: "How is he, Miss Hadlin?"

For some reason she was excited. Frightened, maybe. "He's better," she said. "Miss Ryan and I have been nursing him."

Mary had come into the room behind him, and now she stepped around quickly. "He's a lot better, Leo," she said.

"Maybe I can help nurse him, then," Carver said. He was looking at Ruth and she was white-faced and large-eyed.

Old Pap opened one eye. "Like hell!" he said expressively. "You think I want a reelapse? You get on out of here! Seems like," he protested plaintively, "every time I git to talk to a good-looking gal, somebody comes hornin' in!"

Leo grinned then and looked from Ruth to Mary. "He's in his right mind, anyway," he said, and left.

Mary stood there, looking at Ruth, and Ruth looked after Leo, and then at Mary.

"He's . . . he's an outlaw," Ruth said.

Mary Ryan turned very sharply toward Ruth and I reckon it was the only time she ever spoke up to Ruth. "He's the finest man I ever knew!"

And the two of them just stood there looking at each other and then they went to fussing over Old Pap. That was the longest convalescence on record.

But there was that matter of the blood on her handkerchief. Ruth Hadlin was coming down the street and she was wearing a new bonnet, a beautiful gray dress, and a hat with a veil—very uptown and big city. She was coming down the boardwalk and everybody was turning to look—she was a fine figure of a woman and she carried herself well—and just then the doors of the Palace burst open and out comes a brawling mass of men swinging with all their fists. They spilled past Ruth Hadlin into the street and it turns out to be the three Taylors and Leo Carver.

They hit dirt and came up swinging. Leo smashed a big fist into the face of Scot Taylor and he went over into the street. Bob rushed him, and Leo ducked and took him around the knees, dumping him so hard the ground shook.

Bully Taylor was the tough one, and he and Leo stood there a full half minute, slugging it out with both hands, and then Leo stepped inside and whipped one to Bully's chin and the pride of the Taylors hit dirt, out so cold he's probably sleeping yet.

Ruth Hadlin had stopped in her tracks, and now

Leo stepped back and wiped the blood from his face with a jerk, and some of it splattered on Ruth's handkerchief. She cried out. He turned around, and then he turned colors.

"Miss Hadlin," he said with a grin on his face, "I'm right sorry. I'd no intention getting blood on you, but . . . it's good red blood, even if it isn't blue."

She looked at him without turning a hair, and then she said coolly: "Don't stand there with your face all blood. Go wash it." And then she added just as coolly: "And next time don't lead with your right. If he hadn't been so all in, he'd have knocked you out." With that she walks off up the street and we all stood there staring.

Leo, he stared most of all. "Well, I'm a skinned skunk!" he said. "Where do you reckon she ever heard about leading with a right?"

Mary Ryan, she heard about it, but she said nothing, just nothing at all, and that wasn't Mary's way. Of course, we all knew about Mary. She was plumb crazy about Leo but he paid no particular attention to any one of the girls. Or all of them, for that matter.

There was talk around town, but there always is. Some folks said this was as good a time as any to get shut of Leo Carver and his like. That it was time Cañon Gap changed its ways and spruced up a bit. Mort Lewand was always for changing things. He even wanted to change the name of Cañon Gap to Hadlin. It was the judge himself who stopped that.

So we sat around now and listened to the hammers and thought of how big an occasion it was to be. Some of the folks from the creek were already in town, camped out ready for the big doings tomorrow.

Ruth Hadlin was not around and none of us gave it much thought. All of this was so far away from the Hadlins. Ruth bought a horse, I remember, about that time. It was a fine big black. The 'breed done sold it to her. Funny thing, come to think of it, because I'd heard him turn down $500 for that horse—and that in a country where you get a good horse for $20—but Ruth had ways and nobody refused her very much. What she wanted with a horse that big I never could see.

Editor Chafee, he hoisted his britches and was starting back toward the shop when Ruth Hadlin came down the street. She stopped nearby and she looked at that gallows. Maybe her face was a little pale, but the fact that all those roughnecks were around never seemed to bother her.

"Tom," she said right off, "what do you believe Leo Carver did with that money?"

Chafee rubbed his jaw. "You know"—he scowled—"I've studied about that. I can't rightly say."

"What has he always done with it before?"

"Why, he spent it. Just as fast as he could."

"I wonder why he didn't use it to hire a better lawyer? He could have had a man from El Paso for that. Or for much less. A good lawyer might have freed him."

"I wondered about that." Chafee looked a little anxiously at Mort Lewand. Mort was a power in town and he disliked Carver and made no secret of it. Lewand was looking that way, and now he started over. "It doesn't really matter now, does it?" Chafee added.

Lewand came up and looked from one to the other, then he smiled at Ruth. "Rather noisy, isn't it, Ruth? Would you like me to escort you home?"

"Why, thank you," she said sweetly, "but I think I'll stay. I've never seen a gallows before. Have you, Mister Lewand?"

"Me?" He looked startled. "Oh, yes. In several places."

She stood there a few minutes, watching the carpenters work. "Well," Ruth said slowly, "it's too bad, but I'm glad no local people lost anything in that hold-up."

We all looked at her, but she was watching the gallows, an innocent smile on her lips.

Editor Chafee cleared his throat. "I guess you weren't told, Miss Hadlin. The fact is, that money belonged to Mort, here."

She smiled brightly. Women are strange folk. "Oh, no, Tom. You've been misinformed! As a matter of fact, that money was a payment on Mister Lewand's ranch, and, when he consigned it for carriage, it became the property of the former owner of the ranch. That was the agreement, wasn't it, Mister Lewand?"

For some reason it made Mort mad, but he nodded. "That's right."

Ruth nodded, too. "Yes, Mister Lewand was telling me about it. He's very far-sighted, I think. Isn't that wonderful, Tom? Just think how awful it would have been if he had paid that whole twenty thousand dollars and then lost it and had to pay it over! My, it would take a wealthy man to do that, wouldn't it, now?"

Editor Chafee was looking thoughtful all of a sudden, and Old Pap had taken the pipe from his lips and was staring at Ruth. Mort, he looked mad as a horny toad, though for the life of me, I couldn't see why. After all, it had been a smart stunt.

"Those awful shotguns!" From the way she was talking, you wouldn't have believed that girl had a brain in her head. "I don't believe people should be allowed to own them. I wonder where Leo got the one he used?"

"Claimed he never owned one," Chafee commented slowly.

"He probably borrowed one from a friend," Mort said carelessly. "I suppose they are easy to find."

"That's just it!" Ruth exclaimed. "The man who loaned him that shotgun is just as guilty as he is. I think something should be done about it."

"I doubt if anybody loaned him one," Mort said, off hand. "He probably stole it."

"Oh, no! Because," she added hastily, "if he did, he returned it. Everybody in town who owns a shotgun still has it. There are only six of them in Cañon Gap. Daddy has two, Editor Chafee has one, Pap here has an old broken one, and Mitch always carried one."

"That's only five," Old Pap said softly.

"Oh!" Ruth put her fingers to her mouth. "How silly of me. I'd forgotten yours, Mister Lewand."

There was the silliest silence I ever did hear with nobody looking at anybody else. Suddenly Ruth looked at a little watch she had, gasped something about being late, and started off.

Editor Chafee began to fill his pipe, and Old Pap scratched his knee, and all of us just sat there looking a lot dumber than we were. Mort Lewand didn't seem to know what to say, and what he finally said didn't help much.

"If a man wanted to find a shotgun," he said, "I don't suppose he'd have much trouble." With that he turned and walked off.

You know something? The sound of those hammers wasn't a good sound. Editor Tom Chafee scratched his chin with the stem of his pipe. "Pete," he says to me, "you were supposed to ride shotgun that night. Whose shotgun would you have used?"

"Mitch always lent me his. I was feeling poorly and Mitch took over for me. Leo, he called my name when he first rode up, if you recall."

That shotgun business was bothering all of us. Where *did* Leo get a shotgun? This was a rifle and pistol country, and shotguns just weren't plentiful. Ruth Hadlin could have narrowed it down even more because everybody knew that Judge Hadlin wouldn't let anybody touch one of his guns but himself. They were expensive, engraved guns, and he kept them locked up in a case.

Where had Leo picked up a shotgun? What had he done with the money?

Editor Chafee looked down at Old Pap all of a sudden. "Pap," he said, "let's walk over to my place. You, too, Pete. I want you to look at my shotgun."

We looked at that gun and she was all covered with grease and dust. That shotgun hadn't been fired in six months, anyway. Or for a long time. It certainly hadn't been the gun that killed Mitch and Doc.

"Just for luck," Chafee said seriously, "we'd better have a look at the judge's guns."

Behind us we could hear those hammers a-pounding, and we could hear O'Brien rehearsing his German band. From where we walked, we could see six or seven wagons coming down the road, all headed into Cañon Gap, for the hanging.

Certain things happened that I didn't hear until later. I didn't hear about Ruth Hadlin, all pretty as ever a picture could be, walking into that jail to see Leo Carver. When she got into the office, the sheriff was standing there looking down at a cake on his desk. That cake had been cut and it was some broken up because he had taken two files from it. Mary Ryan was standing by his side.

Sheriff Jones looked mighty serious. "Mary," he was saying, "this here's a criminal offense, helping a man to break jail. Now where's those other two files? No use you stalling. I know you bought four of 'em."

"You're so smart," she said, "you find 'em!" She tossed her head at him and gave him a flash of those saucy eyes of hers.

Sheriff Jones leaned over the table. "Now, look, Mary," he protested, "I don't want to make trouble for you, but we just can't have no prison break. Why, think of all those folks coming for miles to see a hanging! They'd be mad enough to string *me* up."

"Why not?" she said, short-like. "He's no more guilty than you are."

Jones started to protest again, and then he

looked up and saw Ruth Hadlin standing in the door. Her face was cold as she could make it, and, mister, that was cold! In one hand she held Leo's guitar.

The sheriff straightened up mighty flustered. Here he was, talking confidential-like with a girl from the Street! Suppose that got around among the good folks of the town. Be as much as his job was worth, and election coming up, too.

He flushed and stammered. "This here . . . this young woman," he spluttered, "she was trying to smuggle files to the prisoner. She. . . ."

Ruth Hadlin interrupted, her eyes cold and queen-like on the sheriff. "I can assure you, Sheriff Jones, that I am not at all interested in your relations with this young lady, nor in the subject of your conversation. I have brought this guitar to the prisoner," she continued. "I understand he enjoys singing, and we think it cruel and inhuman that he be forced to listen to that banging and hammering while they build a gallows on which to hang him. It is cruel torture."

Jones was embarrassed. "He don't mind, miss," he protested. "Leo, he's. . . ."

"May I take this instrument to him, Sheriff Jones?" Her voice was cold. "Or do you want to examine me? Do you think I might be smuggling files, too?"

Sheriff Jones was embarrassed. The very idea of laying a hand on Ruth Hadlin, the daughter of old Judge Emory Hadlin, gave him cold shivers.

"No, no, miss! Of course not." He gestured toward the cells. "Just you give it to him, miss! I'm sorry. I. . . ."

"Thank you, Sheriff." Ruth swept by him and up to the cell.

"Young man"—her voice was clear—"I understand that you play a guitar so I have brought you this one. I hope the music that you get out of it will make your heart free."

Leo looked startled, and he took the guitar through the bars. "I wish . . . ," he broke off, his face a little flushed. "I wish you didn't have to see me in here. You see, I didn't . . . I never killed those men. I'd like you to believe that."

"What I believe," Ruth said sweetly, "is of no importance. The music from the guitar will be pleasant for you, if played in private." She turned abruptly and walked out, and she went by Sheriff Jones like a pay-car past a tramp.

Mary told it afterwards, and Mary said that Leo plunked a string on that guitar and then he looked at it, funny-like. It sure didn't sound right, Mary said. I shouldn't wonder.

That was late Monday afternoon. By sundown there was maybe 200 people camped around town, waiting for the big hanging next afternoon. Old Pap, he wasn't around, nor was Editor Chafee. Some said that, when they left the judge's house, the judge himself was riding with them.

When next I came across Old Pap, he was standing on the corner, looking at that gallows. That was near the jail, and from the window Leo could see us.

"Folks would be mighty upset if they missed their hanging, Pap," Leo said.

"They won't!" Pap was mighty short and gruff. "They'll git their hanging, and don't you forget it."

That gallows looked mighty ghostly, standing there in the twilight, and it didn't make me feel no better. Leo, well, he always seemed a right nice feller. Of course, he had rustled a few head, but I wouldn't want to take no oath I hadn't, nor Old Pap, nor most of us. Leo, he was just a young hellion, that was all.

Even when he stuck up those stages, he just done it for drinking money. Not that I'm saying it's right, because I know it ain't, but them days and times folks excused a lot of a young man who was full of ginger, long as he didn't hurt nobody and was man enough. Especially of Leo's sort. If you was in trouble you just let him know. Come prairie fire, flood, stampede, or whatever, Leo was your man. No hour was too late, no job too miserable for him to lend a hand. And never take a dime for it.

So we all went to bed, and the last thing Leo said was: "I never did cotton to no rope necktie. I don't figure it's becoming."

"Wait'll tomorry," Old Pap said.

The sun was no more than up before the lid blew off the town. Somebody yelled and folks came a-running. I slid into my pants and scrambled outside. The crowd was streaming toward the Plaza and I run down there with 'em. The bars was out of the jail window, filed off clean as you'd wish, then bent back out of the way. Tied to one of them was a sheet of paper. It was a note.

Sorry I couldn't wait, but I don't think you folks want me hanging around here anyway.

Mary Ryan was there by the jail. She had tears in her eyes, but she looked pleased as a polecat in a hen house, too. Sheriff Jones, he took on something fierce.

"Figured she was talking poetry," he said angrily. "She told him the music he'd get out of the guitar would make his heart free. No wonder Mary wouldn't tell me what became of the other two files."

One big-bearded man with hard eyes stared at the sheriff with a speculative eye. "What about the hanging?" he demanded. "We drove fifty mile to see a hanging."

Editor Tom Chafee, Judge Emory Hadlin, and Old Pap came up around them. They looked across the little circle at Jones.

"Ruth figured it right," the judge said. "Only six shotguns in town. My shotguns, and by the dust on the cases you can see they'd not been cleaned in months. Same with Tom's. Old Pap's was broke, and Mitch had his with him. That leaves just one more shotgun."

Everybody just stood there, taking it all in and doing some figuring. Suppose that $20,000 never left the bank? Or suppose it did leave and it was recovered by the man sending it? His debt would be paid and he would still have the money, and a young scamp like Leo Carver'd be blamed for it all.

Of course, Leo was gone. Some folks said he rode that big black Ruth Hadlin bought. What happened to that horse we never did know because Ruth was gone, too, and her gray mare.

The trail headed west, the trail they left, and

somebody living on the edge of town swore he heard two voices singing something about being bound for Californy.

We figured the judge would about burst a gasket, but he was a most surprising man. Something was said about it by somebody, and all he did was smile a little.

"Many a thoroughbred," he said, "was a frisky colt. Once they get the bridle on 'em, they straighten out. As far as that goes," he added, "every blue-blooded family can use a little red blood!"

So everybody was happy. We celebrated mighty big. I reckon the biggest in the history of Cañon Gap. O'Brien's German band played, and everybody had plenty to eat and drink.

The folks that came for the hanging wasn't disappointed, either. They got what they wanted. They got their hanging, all right. Maybe it wasn't a legal hanging, but it was sure satisfactory.

We hung Mort Lewand.

THE RIDER OF THE RUBY HILLS

Chapter One

There was a lonely place where the trail ran up to the sky. It turned sharply left on the very point of a lofty promontory overlooking the long sweep of the valley below. Here the trail offered to the passerby a vision at this hour. Rosy-tipped peaks and distant purple mountains could be seen, beyond the far reach of the tall-grass range. Upon the very lip of the rocky shelf sat a solitary horseman. He was a man tall in the saddle, astride a strangely marked horse. Its head was held high, its ears were pricked forward with attention riveted upon the valley, as though in tune with the thoughts of its rider. Thoughts that said there lay a new country, with new dangers, new rewards, and new trails.

The rider was a tall man, narrow-hipped and powerful of chest and shoulder. His features were blunt and rugged, so that a watcher might have said: "Here is a man who is not handsome, but a fighter." Yet he was good-looking in his own hard, confident way. He looked now as Cortez might have looked upon a valley in Mexico.

He came alone and penniless, but he did not come as one seeking favors. He did not come hunting a job. He came as a conqueror. For Ross Haney had made his decision. At twenty-seven he was broke. He sat in the middle of all he owned, a splendid Appaloosa gelding, a fine California saddle, a .44 Winchester rifle, and two walnut-stocked Colt .44 pistols. These were his all. Behind him was a life that had taken him from a cradle in a covered wagon to the hurricane deck of many a hard-headed bronco.

It was a life that had left him rich in experience, but poor in goods of the world. The experience was the hard-fisted experience of cold winters, dry ranges, and the dusty bitterness of cattle drives. He had fought Comanches and rustlers, hunted buffalo and horse thieves. Now he was going to ride for himself, to fight for himself.

His keen dark eyes from under the flat black brim of his hat studied the country below with speculative glint. His judgment of terrain would have done credit to a general, and in his own way Ross Haney was a general. His arrival in the Ruby Valley country was in its way an invasion.

He was a young man with a purpose. He did not want wealth but a ranch, a well-watered ranch in a good stock country. That his pockets were empty did not worry him, for he had made up his mind, and, as men had discovered before this, Ross Haney with his mind made up was a force to be reckoned with. Nor was he riding blindly into a strange land. Like a good tactician he had gathered his information carefully, judged the situation, the terrain, and the enemy before he began his move.

This was a new country to him, but he knew the landmarks and the personalities. He knew the strength and the weaknesses of its rulers, knew the economic factors of their existence, knew the stresses and the strains within it. He knew that he rode into a valley at war—that blood had been shed, and that armed men rode its trails day and night. Into this land he rode a man alone, determined to have his own from the country, come what may, letting the chips fall where they might.

With a movement of his body he turned the gelding left down the trail into the pines, a trail where at this late hour it would soon be dark, a trail somber, majestic in its stillness under the columned trees.

As he moved under the trees, he removed his hat and rode slowly. It was good country, a country where a man could live and grow, and where, if he was lucky, he might have sons to grow tall and straight beside him. This he wanted. He wanted his own hearth fire, the creak of his own pump, the heads of his own horses looking over the gate bars for his hand to feed them. He wanted peace, and for it he came to a land at war.

A flicker of light caught his eye, and the faint smell of wood smoke. He turned the gelding toward the fire, and, when he was near, he swung down. The sun's last rays lay bright through the pines upon this spot. The earth was trampled by hoofs, and in the fire itself the ashes were gray but for one tiny flame that thrust a bright spear upward from the end of a stick.

Studying the scene, his eyes held for an instant on one place where the parched grass had been blackened in a perfect ring. His eyes glinted with hard humor. *A cinch-ring artist. Dropped her there to cool and she singed the grass. A pretty smooth gent, I'd say.* Not slick enough, of course. A smarter man, or a less confident one, would have pulled up that handful of blackened grass and tossed it into the flames.

There had been two men here, his eyes told him. Two men and two horses. One of the men had been a big man with small feet. The impressions of his feet were deeper and he had mounted the largest horse.

Curious, he studied the scene. This was a new country for him and it behooved a man to know the local customs. He grinned at the thought. If cinch-ring branding was one of the local customs, it was a strange one. In most sections of the country the activity was frowned upon, to say the least. If an artist was caught pursuing his calling, he was likely to find himself at the wrong end of a hair rope with nothing under his feet.

The procedure was simple enough. One took a cinch ring from his own saddle gear and, holding it between a couple of sticks, used it when red-hot like any other branding iron. A good hand with a cinch ring could easily duplicate any known brand, depending only upon his degree of skill.

Ross rolled and lighted a smoke. If he were found on the spot, it would require explaining, and at the moment he had no intention of explaining anything. He swung his leg over the saddle and turned the gelding downtrail once more.

Not three miles away lay the cow town known as Soledad. To his right, and about six miles away, was an imposing cluster of buildings shaded beneath a splendid grove of old cottonwoods. Somewhat nearer, and also well-shaded, was a smaller ranch.

Beyond the rocky ridge that stretched an anxious finger into the lush valley was Walt Pogue's Box N spread. The farther ranch belonged to Chalk Reynolds, his RR outfit being easily the biggest in the Ruby Hills country. The nearer ranch belonged to Bob and Sherry Vernon.

"When thieves fall out," Ross muttered aloud, "honest men get their dues. Or that's what they say. Now I'm not laying any claim to being so completely honest, but there's trouble brewing in this valley. When the battle smoke blows away, Ross Haney is going to be top dog on one of those ranches. They've got it all down there. They have range, money, power. They have gun hands riding for them, but you and me, Río, we've only got each other."

He was a lone wolf on the prowl. Down there they ran in packs, and he would circle the packs, alone. When the moment came, he would close in.

"There's an old law, Río, that only the strong survive," he said. "Those ranches belong to men who were strong, and some of them still are. They were strong enough to take them from other men, from smaller men, weaker men. That's the story of Reynolds and Pogue. They rustled cows until they grew big and now they sit on the housetops and crow. Or they did until they began fightin' one another."

"Your reasoning"—the cool, quiet voice was feminine—"is logical, but dangerous. I might suggest that, when you talk to your horse, you should be sure his are the only ears!"

She sat well in the saddle, poised and alert. There was a quirk of humor at the corners of her mouth, and nothing of coyness or fear in her manner. Every inch of her showed beauty, care, and consideration of appearances that were new to him, but beneath them there were both fire and steel—and quality.

"That's good advice," he agreed, measuring her with his eyes. "Very good advice."

"Now that you've looked me over," she suggested coolly, "would you like to examine my teeth for age?"

He grinned, unabashed. "No, but now that I've looked you over, I'd say you are pretty much of a woman. The kind that's made for a man!"

She returned his glance, then smiled as if the remark had pleased her. So she changed the subject. "Just which ranch do you plan to be top dog on when the fighting is over?"

"I haven't decided," he said frankly. "I'm a right choosy sort of man when it comes to horses, ranches, and women!"

"Yes?" She glanced at the gelding. "I'd say your judgment of horses isn't obvious by that one. Not that he isn't well-shaped, and I imagine he could run, but you could do better."

"I doubt it." He glanced at her fine, clean-limbed thoroughbred. "I'd bet a little money he can outrun that beauty of yours, here to Soledad."

Her eyes flashed. "Why, you idiot! Flame is the

fastest horse in this country. He comes of racing stock!"

"I don't doubt it," Haney agreed. "He's a fine horse. But I'll bet my saddle against a hundred dollars that this Appaloosa will kick dust in his face before we get to Soledad!"

She laughed scornfully, and her head came up. "You're on!" she cried, and her red horse gave a great bound and hit the trail running. That jump gave the bay the start, but Ross knew his gelding.

Leaning over, he yelled into the horse's ear as they charged after the bay: "Come on, boy! We've got to beat that bay! We need the money!" And Río, seeming to understand, stretched his legs and ran like a scared rabbit.

As they swept into the main road and in full sight of Soledad, the bay was leading by three lengths, but despite the miles behind it, the Appaloosa loved to run, and he was running now.

The gelding had blood of Arabians in his veins, and he was used to off-hand, cow camp style racing. The road took a small jog, but Ross did not swing the gelding around it, but took the desert and mountain-bred horse across the stones and through the mesquite, hitting the road scarcely a length behind the big red horse.

Men were gathering in the street and on the edge of town now and shouting about the racing horses. With a half mile to go the big red horse was slowing. He was a sprinter, but he had been living too well with too little running. The gelding was just beginning to run. Neck stretched, Ross leaning far forward to cut the wind resistance and lend impetus with his weight, the mustang thundered alongside the bay horse, and neck and neck they raced up to the town. Then, with the nearest building only a short jump ahead, Ross Haney spoke to the Appaloosa: *"Now,* Río! *Now!"*

With a lunge, the spotted horse was past and went racing into the street leading by a length.

Ross eased back on the reins and let the horse run on down the street abreast of the big red horse. They slowed to a canter, then a walk. The girl's eyes were wide and angry.

"You cheated! You cut across that bend!"

Ross chuckled. "You could have, miss! And you got off to a running start. Left me standing still!"

"I thought you wanted a race!" she protested scornfully. "You cheated me!"

Ross Haney drew up sharply, and his eyes went hard. "I reckon, ma'am," he said, "you come from a long line of sportsmen! You can forget the bet!"

The sarcasm in his voice cut like a whip. She opened her mouth to speak, but he had turned the Appaloosa away and was walking it back toward the center of town.

For an instant, she started to follow, and then with a toss of her head, she let him go.

Chapter Two

Several men were standing in front of the livery stable when he rode up. They looked at his horse, then at him. "That's a runner you got there, stranger! I reckon Sherry Vernon didn't relish getting beat! She sets great store by the Flame horse!"

Haney swung down and led the horse into the stable where he rubbed him down and fed him. As he worked, he thought over what he had just learned. The girl was Sherry Vernon, one of the owners of the Twin V spread, and she had overheard his meditations on his plans. How seriously she would take them would be something else again. Well, it did not matter. He was planning no subterfuge. He had come to Ruby Valley on the prod, and they could find it out now as well as later.

The girl had been beautiful. That stuck in his mind after he thought of all the rest. It was the feeling that hung over his thinking with a certain aura that disturbed him. He had known few women who affected him, and those few had been in New Orleans or Kansas City on his rare trips there. Yet this one touched a chord that had answered to none of the others.

Suddenly he was conscious of a looming figure beside him. For a moment he continued to work. Then he looked around into a broad, handsome face. The man was smiling.

"My name's Pogue," he said, thrusting out a hand. "Walt Pogue. I own the Box N. Is that horse for sale?"

"No, he's not."

"I'd not figured you'd be willing to sell. If you get that idea, come look me up. I'll give you five hundred for him."

$500? That was a lot of money in a country full of ten-dollar mustangs or where a horse was often traded for a quart of whiskey.

"No," Haney repeated, "he's not for sale."

"Lookin' for a job? I could use a hand."

Ross Haney drew erect and looked over the horse's back. He noticed, and the thought somehow irritated him, that Pogue was even bigger than himself. The rancher was all of three inches taller and forty pounds heavier. And he did not look fat.

"Gun hand? Or cowhand?"

Walt Pogue's eyes hardened a shade, and then he smiled, a grim knowing smile. "Why, man," he said softly, "that would depend on you. But if you hire on as a warrior, you've got to be good!"

"I'm good. As good as any you've got."

"As good as Bob Streeter or Repp Hanson?"

Ross Haney's expression made no change, but within him he felt something tighten up and turn hard and wary. If Pogue had hired Streeter and Hanson, this was going to be ugly. Both men were killers, and not particular how they worked or how they killed.

"As good as Streeter or Hanson?" Haney shrugged. "A couple of cheap killers. Blood hunters. They aren't fighting men." His dark eyes met that searching stare of Walt Pogue again. "Who does Reynolds have?"

Pogue's face seemed to lower and he stared back at Haney. "He's got Emmett Chubb."

Emmett Chubb! So? And after all these years? "He won't have him long," Haney said, "because I'm going to kill him!"

Triumph leaped in Pogue's eyes. Swiftly he moved around the horse. "Haney," he said, "that job could get you an even thousand dollars."

"I don't take money for killing snakes."

"You do that job within three days and you'll get a thousand dollars," Pogue said flatly.

Ross Haney pushed by the big man without replying and walked into the street. Three men sat on the rail by the stable door. Had they heard what was said inside? He doubted it, and yet?

Across the street and three doors down was the Trail Emporium. For a long moment his eyes held their look at the one light gleaming in the back of the store. It was after hours and the place was closed, but at the back door there might be a chance. Deliberately he stepped into the street and crossed toward the light.

Behind him Walt Pogue moved into the doorway and stared after him, his brow furrowed with thought. His eyes went down the lean, powerful figure of the strange rider with a puzzled expression. Who was he? Where had he come from? Why was he here? He wore two well-worn, tied-down guns. He had the still, remote face and the careful eyes typical of a man who had lived much with danger, and typical of so many of the gunfighters of the West. He had refused, or avoided the offer of a job, yet he had seemed well aware of conditions in the valley. Had Reynolds sent for him? Or Bob Vernon? He had ridden into town racing with Sherry. Had they met on the trail, or come from the VV? That Pogue must know and at once. If Bob Vernon was hiring gun hands, it would mean trouble, and that he did not want. One thing at a time. Where was he going now? Resisting an instinct to follow Haney, Pogue turned and walked up the street toward the Bit and Bridle Saloon.

Haney walked up to the back door of the store building, hesitated an instant, then tapped lightly.

Footsteps sounded within, and he heard the sound of a gun being drawn from a scabbard. "Who's there?"

Haney spoke softly. "A rider from the Pecos."

The door opened at once, and Ross slid through the opening. The man who faced him was round and white-haired. Yet the eyes that took Haney in from head to heel were not old eyes. They were shrewd, hard, and knowing.

"Coffee?"

"Sure. Food, if you got some ready."

"About to eat myself." The man placed the gun on a sideboard and lifted the coffee pot from the stove. He filled the cup as Ross dropped into a chair. "Who sent you here?"

Haney glanced up, then tipped back in his chair. "Don't get on the prod, old-timer. I'm friendly. When an old friend of yours heard I was headed this way, and might need a smart man to give me a word of advice, he told me to look you up. And he told me what to say to you, Scott."

"My days on that trail are over."

"Mine never started. This is a business trip. I'm planning to locate in the valley."

"Locate? Here?" The older man stared at him. He filled his own cup, and, dishing up a platter of food and slapping bread on a plate, he sat down. "You came to me for advice. All right, you'll get it. Get on your horse and ride out of here as fast as you can. This is no country for strangers, and there have been too many of them around. Things are due to bust wide open and there will be a sight of killin' before it's over."

"You're right, of course."

"Sure. An' after it's over, what's left for a gun hand? You can go on the owlhoot, that's all. The very man who hired you and paid you warrior's wages won't want you when the fighting is over. There's revolution coming in this country. If you know the history of revolutions, you'll know that as soon as one is over the first thing they do is liquidate the revolutionists. You ride out of here."

Ross Haney ate in silence. The older man was right. To ride out would be the intelligent, sensible, and safe course, and he had absolutely no intention of doing it.

"Scott, I didn't come here to hire on as a gun hand. In fact, I have already had an offer. I came into this country because I've sized it up and I know what it's like. This country can use a good man, a strong man. There's a place for me here, and I mean to take it. Also, I want a good ranch. I aim to settle down, and I plan to get my ranch the same way Pogue, Reynolds, and the rest of them got theirs."

"Force? You mean with a gun?" Scott was incredulous. "Listen, young fellow, Pogue has fifty riders on his range, and most of them are ready to fight at the drop of a hat. Reynolds has just as many, and maybe more. And you come in here alone . . . or are you alone?"

The storekeeper bent a piercing gaze upon the young man, who smiled.

"I'm alone." Haney shrugged. "Scott, I've been fighting for existence ever since I was big enough to walk. I've fought to hold other people's cattle, fought for other men's homes, fought for the lives of other men. I've worked and bled and sweated my heart out in rain, dust, and storm. Now I want something for myself. Maybe I came too late. Maybe I'm 'way off the trail. But it seems to me that, when trouble starts, a man might stand on the sidelines, and, when the time comes, he might move in. You see, I know how Walt Pogue got his ranch. Vin Carter was a friend of mine until Emmett Chubb killed him. He told me how Pogue forced his old man off his range and took over. Well, I happen to know that none of this range is legally held. It's been preëmpted, which gives them a claim, of course. Well, I've got a few ideas myself. And I'm moving in."

"Son"—Scott leaned across the table—"listen to me. Pogue's the sort of man who would hire killers by the hundreds if he had to. He did force Carter off his range. He did take it by force, and he has held it by force. Now he and Chalk are in a battle over who is to keep it, and which one is to come out on top. The Vernons are the joker in the deck. What both Reynolds and Pogue want is the Vernon place because whoever holds it has a grip on this country. But both of them are taking the Vernons too lightly. They have something up their sleeve, or somebody has."

"What do you mean?"

"There's this Star Levitt, for one. He's no soft touch, that one! And then he's got some riders around there, and I'd say they do more work for him than for the Vernon spread . . . and not all honest work, by any means."

"Levitt a Western man?"

"He could be. Probably is. But whoever he is, he knows his way around an' he's one sharp *hombre*. Holds his cards close to his chest, an' plays 'em that way. He's the one you've got to watch in this deal, not Reynolds or Pogue."

Ross Haney leaned back in his chair and smiled at Scott. "That meal sure tasted good," he acknowledged. "Now comes the rough part. I want to borrow some money . . . military funds," he added, grinning.

Scott shook his white head. "You sure beat all! You come into this country huntin' trouble, all alone, an' without money! You've got nerve! I only hope you've got the gun savvy and the brains to back it up." The blue eyes squinted from his leather brown face and he smiled. He was beginning to like Haney. The tall young man had humor and the nerve of the project excited and amused the old outlaw. "How much do you want?"

"A hundred dollars."

"That all? You won't get far in this country on that."

"No, along with it I want some advice." Haney hitched himself forward and took a bit of paper from his pocket, then a stub of pencil. Then from a leather folder he took a larger sheet that he unfolded carefully. It was a beautifully tanned piece of calfskin, and on it was drawn a map. Carefully he moved the dishes aside and placed it on the table facing the older man. "Look that over and, if you see any mistakes, correct me."

Scott stared at the map, then he leaned forward, his eyes indicating his amazed interest. It was a map, drawn to scale and in amazing detail, of the Ruby Hills country. Every line camp, every water hole, every ranch, and every stand of trees was indicated plainly. Distances were marked on straight lines between the various places, and heights of land. Lookout points were noted, cañons indicated. Studying the map, Scott could find nothing it had missed.

Slowly he leaned back in his chair. When he looked up, his expression was halfway between respect and worry. "Son, where did you get that map?"

"Get it? I made it. I drew it myself, Scott. For three years I've talked to every 'puncher or other man I've met from this country. As they told me stuff, I checked with others and built this map. You know how Western men are. Most of them are pretty good at description. A man down in the Live Oaks country who never left it knows how the sheriff looks in Julesberg, and exactly where the corrals are in Dodge." Haney took a deep breath, then continued his story. "Well, I've been studying this situation quite a spell. An old buffalo hunter and occasional trapper was in this country once, and he told me about it when I was a kid. It struck me as a place I'd like to live, so I planned accordingly. I learned all I could about it, rode for outfits oftentimes just because some 'puncher on the spread had worked over here. Then I ran into Vin Carter. He was born here. He told me all about it, and I got more from him than any of them. While I was riding north with a herd of cattle, Emmett Chubb moved in, picked a fight with the kid, and killed him. And I think Walt Pogue paid him to do it. So it goes further than the fact that I'm range hungry, and I'll admit I am. I want my own spread. But Vin rode with me and we fought sandstorms and blizzards together from Texas to Montana and back. So I'm a man on the prod. Before I get through, I'll own me a ranch in this country, a nice ranch with nice buildings, and then I'll get a wife and settle down."

Scott's eyes glinted. "It's a big order, son, Gosh, if I was twenty years younger, I'd throw in with you. I sure would."

"There's no man I'd want more, Scott, but this is my fight, and I'll make it alone. You can stake me to eating money, if you want, and I'll need some Forty-Four cartridges."

The older man nodded assent. "You can have them, an' willin'. Have you got a plan?"

Haney nodded. "It's already started. I've filed on Thousand Springs."

Scott came off his chair, his face a mask of incredulity. "You *what?*"

"I filed a claim, an' I've staked her out and started to prove up." Ross was smiling over his coffee, enjoying Scott's astonishment.

"But, man! That's sheer suicide! That's right in the middle of Chalk's best range! That water hole is worth a fortune. A dozen fortunes. That's what half the fighting is about."

"I know it." Haney was calm. "I knew that before I came in here. That Appaloosa of mine never moved a step until I had my plan of action all staked out. And I bought the Bullhorn."

This time astonishment was beyond the storekeeper. "How could you buy it? Gov'ment land, ain't it?"

"No. That's what they all think. Even Vin Carter thought so, but it was part of a Spanish Grant. I found that out by checking through some old records. So I hunted up a Mex down in the Big Bend country who owned it. I bought it from him, bought three hundred acres, taking in the whole Bullhorn headquarters spread, the water hole, and the cliffs in back of it. That includes most of that valley where Pogue cuts his meadow hay."

"Well, I'm forever bushed. If that don't beat all." Scott tapped thoughtfully with his pipe bowl. Then he looked up. "What about Hitson Spring?"

"That's another thing I want to talk to you about. You own it."

"I do, eh? How did you come to think that?"

"Met an old sidewinder down in Laredo named Smite Emmons. He was pretty drunk one night in a greaser's shack, and he told me how foolish you were to file claim on that land. Said you could have bought it from the Indians just as cheap."

Scott chuckled. "I did. I bought it from the Indians, too. Believe me, son, nobody around here knows that. It would be a death sentence."

"Then sell it to me. I'll give you my note for five hundred right now."

"Your note, eh?" Scott chuckled. "Son, you'd better get killed. It will be cheaper to bury you than pay up." He tapped his pipe bowl again. "Tell you what I'll do. I'll take your note for five hundred and the fun of watching what happens."

Solemnly Ross Haney wrote out a note, and handed it to Scott. The old man chuckled as he read it.

> I hereby agree to pay on or before the 15th of March, 1877, to Westbrook Scott, the sum of $500 and the fun of watching what happens for the 160 acres of land known as Hitson Spring.

"All right, son. Sign her up. I'll get you the deed."

Chapter Three

When Ross had pocketed the two papers, the deed from the government to Scott and deeded over to him, and the skin deed from the Comanches, the old man sat up and reached for the coffee pot.

"You know what you've done? You've got a claim on the three best sources of water in Ruby Valley, the only three that are sure-fire all the year around. And what will they do when they find out? They'll kill you!"

"They won't find out for a while. I'm not talking until the fight's been taken out of them."

"What about your claim stakes at Thousand Springs?"

"Buried. Iron stakes, and driven deep into the ground. There's sod and grass over the top."

"What about proving up?"

"That, too. You know how that spring operates? Actually it is one great big spring back inside the mountain, flowing out through the rocky face of the cliff in hundreds of tiny rivulets. Well, atop the mesa there is a good piece of land that falls into my claim, and back in the woods there is some land I can plow. I've already broken that land, smoothed her out, and put in a crop. I've got a trail to the top of that mesa, and a stone house built up there. I'm in business, Scott!"

Scott looked at him and shook his head. Then he pushed back from the table and, getting up, went into the store. When he returned, he had several boxes of shells.

"In the mornin' come around and stock up," he suggested. "You better make you a cache or two with an extra gun here and there, and some extra ammunition. Maybe a little grub. Be good insurance, and, son, you'll need it."

"That's good advice. I'll do it, an' you keep track of the expense. I'll settle every cent of it when this is over."

With money in his pocket he walked around the store and crossed the street to the Bit and Bridle. The bartender glanced at him, then put a bottle and a glass in front of him. He was a short man, very thick and fat, but, after a glance at the corded forearms, Ross was very doubtful about it all being fat.

A couple of lazy-talking cowhands held down the opposite end of the bar, and there was a poker game in progress at a table. Several other men sat around on chairs. They were the usual nondescript crowd of the cow trails.

He poured his drink, and had just taken it between his thumb and fingers when the bat-wing doors thrust open and he heard the click of heels behind him. He neither turned nor looked around. The amber liquid in the glass held his attention. He had never been a drinking man, taking only occasional shots, and he was not going to drink much tonight.

The footsteps halted abreast of him, and a quick, clipped voice said in very precise words: "Are you the chap who owns that fast horse, the one with the black forequarters and the white over the loin and hips?"

He glanced around, turning his head without moving his body. There was no need to tell him that this was Bob Vernon. He was a tall, clean-limbed young man who was like her in that imperious lift to his chin, unlike her in his quick, decisive manner.

"There's spots, egg-shaped black spots over the white," said Haney. "That the one you mean?"

"My sister is outside. She wants to speak to you."

"I don't want to speak to her. You can tell her that." He turned his attention to his drink.

What happened then happened so fast it caught him off balance. A hand grasped him by the shoulder and spun him around in a grip of iron, and he was conscious of being surprised at the strength in that slim hand. Bob Vernon was staring at him, his eyes blazing.

"I said my sister wanted to speak to you!"

"And I said I didn't want to speak to her." Ross Haney's voice was slow-paced and even. "Now take your hand off me and don't ever lay a hand on me again."

Bob Vernon was a man who had never backed down for anyone. From the East he had come into the cow country of Ruby Valley and made a place for himself by energy, decision, and his own youthful strength. Yet he had never met a man such as he faced now. As he looked into the hard eyes of the stranger, he felt something turn over deeply inside him. It was as though he had parted the brush and looked into the face of a lion.

Vernon dropped his hand. "I'm sorry. I'm afraid your manner made me forgetful. My sister can't come into a place like this."

The two men measured each other, and the suddenly alert audience in the Bit and Bridle let their eyes go from Vernon to the stranger. Bob Vernon they knew well enough to know he was afraid of nothing that walked. They also knew his normal manner was polite to a degree rarely encountered in the West where manners were inclined to be brusque, friendly, and lacking in formality. Yet there was something else between these two now. As one man they seemed to sense the same intangible something that had touched Bob Vernon.

The bat-wing doors parted suddenly, and Sherry Vernon stepped into the room.

First, Haney was aware of a shock that such a girl could come into such a place, and, second, of shame that he had been the cause. Then he felt admiration sweep over him at her courage.

Beautiful in a gray, tailored riding habit, her head lifted proudly, she walked up to Ross Haney. Her face was set and her eyes were bright.

Ross was suddenly conscious that never in all his life had he looked into eyes so fine, so filled with feeling.

"Sir"—and her voice could be heard in every corner of the room—"I do not know what your name may be, but I have come to pay you your money. Your horse beat Flame today, and beat him fairly. I regret the way I acted, but it was such a shock to have Flame beaten that I allowed you to get away without being paid. I am very sorry. "However," she added quickly, "if you would like to run against Flame again, I'll double the bet."

"Thank you, Miss Vernon." He bowed slightly, from the hips. "It was only that remark about my horse that made me run him at all. You see, miss, as you no doubt know, horses have feelin's. I couldn't let you run down my horse to his face thataway!"

Her eyes were on his and, suddenly, they crinkled at the corners and her lips rippled with a little smile.

"Now, if you'll allow me. . . ." He took her arm and escorted her from the room. Inside, they heard a sudden burst of applause, and he smiled as he offered her his hands for her foot. She stepped into them, then swung into her position on the horse.

"I'm sorry you had to come in there, but your brother was kind of abrupt."

"That's quite all right," she replied quickly, almost too quickly. "Now our business is completed."

He stepped back and watched them ride away into the darkness of early evening. Then he turned back to the saloon. He almost ran into a tall, carefully dressed man who had walked up behind him. A man equally as large as Pogue.

Pale blue eyes looked from a handsome, perfectly cut face of city white. He was trim, neat, and precise. Only the guns at his hips looked deadly with their polished butts and worn holsters.

"That," said the tall man, gesturing after Sherry Vernon, "is a staked claim!"

Ross Haney was getting angry. Men who were bigger than he always irritated him, anyway. "If you think you can stake a claim on any woman, you've got a lot to learn."

He shoved by toward the door, but behind him the voice said: "But that one's staked. You hear me?"

Soledad by night was a tiny scattering of lights along the dark river of the street. Music from the tinny piano in the Bit and Bridle drifted down the street, and with it the lazy voice of someone singing a cow camp song. Ross Haney turned up the street toward the two-story frame hotel, his mind unable to free itself from the vision that was Sherry Vernon.

For the first time, the wife who was to share that ranch had a face. Until now there had been in his thoughts the vague shadow of a personality and a character, but there had been no definite features, nothing that could be recognized. Now, after seeing Sherry, he knew there could be but one woman in the ranch house he planned to build.

He smiled wryly as he thought of her sharing his life. What would she think of a cowhand? A drifting gun hand? And what would she say when it became known that he was Ross Haney? Not that the name meant very much, for it did not. Only, in certain quarters where fighting men gather, he had acquired something of a reputation. The stories about him had drifted across the country as such stories will, and, while he had little notoriety as a gunfighter, he was known as a hard, capable man who would and could fight.

He was keenly aware of his situation in Soledad and the Ruby Hills country. As yet, he was an outsider. They were considering him, and Pogue had already sensed enough of what he was to offer a job, gun or saddle job. When his intentions became known, he would be facing trouble and plenty of it. When they discovered that he had actually moved in and taken possession of the best water in the valley, they would have no choice but to buy him out, run him out, or kill him. Or they could move out themselves, and neither Walt Pogue nor Chalk Reynolds was the man for that.

In their fight Ross had no plan to take sides. He was a not too innocent bystander as far as they were concerned. When Bob and Sherry Vernon were considered, he wasn't too sure. He scowled, realizing suddenly that sentiment had no place in such dealings as his. Until he saw Sherry Vernon, he had been a free agent, and now, for better or worse, he was no longer quite so free.

He could not now move with such cold indifference to the tides of war in the Ruby Hills. Now he had an interest, and his strength was lowered to just the degree of that interest. He was fully aware of the fact. It nettled him even as it amused him, for he was always conscious of himself, and viewed his motives with a certain wry, ironic humor, seeing himself always with much more clarity than others saw him.

Yet, despite that, something had been accomplished. He had staked his claim at Thousand Springs, and started his cabin. He had talked with Scott, and won an ally there, for he knew the old man was with him, at least to a point. He had met and measured Walt Pogue, and he knew that Emmett Chubb was now with Reynolds. That would take some investigation, for from all he had learned he had been sure that Pogue had hired Chubb to kill Vin Carter, but now Chubb worked for Reynolds.

Well, the alliance of such men was tied to a dollar sign, and their loyalty was no longer than their next pay day. And there might have been trouble between Pogue and Chubb, and that might be the reason Pogue was so eager to have him killed.

He directed his thoughts toward the Vernons. Bob was all man. Whatever Reynolds and Pogue planned for him, he would not take. He would have his own ideas, and he was a fighter.

What of the other hands who Scott implied were loyal to Levitt rather than Vernon? These men he must consider, too, and must plan carefully for them, for in such an action as he planned, he must be aware of all the conflicting elements in the valley.

The big man in the white hat he had placed at once. Carter had mentioned him with uncertainty, for when Carter left the valley Star Levitt had just arrived and was an unknown quantity.

With that instinctive awareness that the widely experienced man has for such things, Ross Haney knew that he and Star Levitt were slated to be enemies. They were two men who simply could not be friends, for there was a definite clash of personalities and character that made a physical clash inevitable. And Haney was fully aware that Star Levitt was not the soft touch some might believe. He was a dangerous man, a very dangerous man.

Chapter Four

Ross Haney found the Cattleman's Rest Hotel was a long building with thirty rooms, a large empty lobby, and off to one side a restaurant. Feeling suddenly hungry, he turned to the desk for a room, his eyes straying toward the restaurant door.

When Haney dropped his war bag, a young man standing in the doorway turned and walked to the desk. "Room?" He smiled as he spoke, and his face was pleasant.

"The best you've got." Ross grinned at him.

The clerk grinned back. "Sorry, but they are all equally bad, even if reasonably clean. Take Fifteen at the end of the hall. You'll be closer to the well."

"Pump?"

The clerk chuckled. "What do you think this is? New York? It's a rope and bucket well. It's been almost a year since we hauled a dead man out of it. The water should be good by now."

"Sure." Ross studied him for a moment. "Where you from? New York?"

"Yes, and Philadelphia, Boston, Richmond, London, and San Francisco, and now . . . Soledad."

"You've been around." Ross rolled a smoke and dropped the sack on the desk for the clerk. "How's the food?"

"Good. Very good . . . and the prettiest waitress west of the Mississippi."

Ross smiled. "Well, if she's like the other girls around here, she's probably a staked claim. I had a big *hombre* with a white hat tell me tonight that one girl was staked out for him."

The clerk looked at him quickly, shrewdly. "Star Levitt?"

"I guess."

"If he meant the lady you had the race with today, I'd say he was doing more hoping than otherwise. Sherry Vernon"—the clerk spoke carefully—"is not an easy claim to stake."

Ross pulled the register around, hesitated an instant, and then wrote his name: Ross Haney, El Paso.

The clerk glanced at it, then looked up. "Glad to meet you, Ross. My name is Allan Kinney." He looked down at the name again. "Ross Haney. I've heard that name from somewhere. It's funny," he added musingly, "about a name and a town. Ross Haney, from El Paso. Now you might not be from El Paso at all. You might be from Del Río or Sanderson or Uvalde. You might even be from Cheyenne or from Fort Sumner or White Oaks. What happened to you in El Paso? Or wherever you came from? And why did you come here? Men drift without reason sometimes, but usually there is something. Sometimes the law is behind them, or an outlaw ahead of them. Sometimes they just want new horizons or a change of scene, and sometimes they are hunting for something. You, now, I'd say you had come to Soledad for a reason . . . a reason that could mean trouble."

"Let's drink some coffee," Haney suggested, "and see if that waitress is as pretty as you say."

"You won't think so," Kinney said, shaking his head, "you won't think so at all. You've just seen Sherry Vernon. After her all women looked washed out . . . until you get over her."

"I don't plan on it."

The two men entered the restaurant and selected a table. Kinney dropped into a chair. "That, my friend, is a large order. Miss Vernon usually handles such situations with neatness and dispatch. She is always pleasant, never familiar."

"This is different." Ross, seated now, looked up and suddenly he knew with a queer excitement just what he was going to say. He said it. "I'm going to marry her."

Allan Kinney gulped. "Have you told her? Does she know your intentions are honorable? Does she even know you have intentions?" He grinned. "You know, friend, that is a large order you have laid out for yourself."

The waitress came up. She was a slender, very pretty girl with red hair, a few freckles, and a sort of bubbling good humor that was contagious.

"May," Kinney said, "I want you to meet Ross Haney. He is going to marry Sherry Vernon."

At this Ross felt his ears getting red and cursed himself for a thick-headed fool for ever saying such a thing. It may have been startled from him by the sudden realization that he intended to do just that.

"What?" May said quickly, looking at him, "another one?"

Haney glanced up and suddenly he put his hand over hers and said gently: "No, May. *The* one!"

Her eyes held his for a moment, and the laughter faded from them. "You know," she said seriously, "I think you might!"

She went for their coffee. Kinney looked at Ross with care. "Friend Haney," he said, "you have made an impression. I really think the lady believed you. Now if you can do as well with Miss Vernon, you'll be doing all right."

The door opened suddenly from the street and two men stepped in. Ross glanced up, and his dark eyes held on the two men who stood there. One of the men was a big man with sloping shoulders, and his eyes caught Haney's and narrowed as if in sudden recognition. The other man was shorter, thicker, but obviously a hardcase. Ross guessed that these men were from the Vernon ranch—or they could be, riders at least who knew about Ross Haney and were more than casually interested. These could be the men who worked for Star Levitt, and as such they merited study, yet their type was not an unfamiliar one to Ross Haney, or to any man who rode the borderlands or the wild country. While many a cowpuncher has branded a few mavericks or rustled a few cows when he needed drinking money, or wanted a new saddle, there was a certain intangible, yet very real difference that marked those who held to the outlaw trail, and both of these men had it. They were men with guns for hire, men who rode for trouble, and for the ready cash they could get for crooked work. He knew their type. He had faced such men before, and he knew they recognized him. These men were a type who never fought a battle for anyone but themselves.

No sooner were these two seated than May brought their coffee. Then, without warning, the door pushed open again and two more men came into the room. Ross glanced around and caught the eye of a short, stocky man who walked with a quick, jerky lift of his knees. He walked now—right over to Haney.

"You're Ross Haney?" he said abruptly. "I've got a job for you! Start tomorrow morning! A hundred a month an' found. Plenty of horses! I'm Chalk Reynolds an' my place is just out of town in that big clump of cottonwoods. Old place. You won't have any trouble finding it."

Ross smiled. "Sorry, I'm not hunting a job."

Reynolds had been turning away; he whipped back quickly. "What do you mean? Not looking for a job? At a hundred a month? When the range is covered with top hands gettin' forty?"

"I said I didn't want a job."

"Ah?" The genial light left the older man's face, and his blue eyes hardened and narrowed. "So that's it! You've gone to work for Walt Pogue!"

"No, I don't work for Pogue. I don't work for anybody. I'm my own man, Mister Reynolds."

Chalk Reynolds stared at him. "Listen, my friend, and listen well. In the Ruby Hills today there are but two factions, those for Reynolds, and those against him. If you don't work for me, I'll regard you as an enemy."

Haney shrugged. "That's your funeral. From all I hear you have enemies enough without choosing any more. Also, from all I hear, you deserve them."

"What?" Reynolds's eyes blazed. "Don't sass me, stranger!"

The lean, whip-bodied man beside him touched his arm. "Let me handle this, Uncle Chalk," he said gently. "Let me talk to this man."

Ross shifted his eyes. The younger man had a lantern jaw and unusually long gray eyes. The eyes had a flatness about them that puzzled and warned him. "My name is Sydney Berdue. I am foreman for Mister Reynolds." He stepped closer to where Haney sat in his chair, one elbow on the table. "Maybe you would like to tell me why he deserves his enemies."

Haney glanced up at him, his blunt features composed, faintly curious, his eyes steady and aware. "Sure," he said quietly. "I'd be glad to. Chalk Reynolds came West from Missouri right after the war with Mexico. For a time he was located in Santa Fé, but, as the wagon trains started to come West, he went north and began selling guns to the Indians."

Reynolds's face went white and his eyes blazed. "That's not true!"

Haney's glance cut his words short. "Don't make me kill you," Ross said sharply. "Every word I say is true. You took part in wagon train raids yourself. I expect you collected your portion of white scalps. Then you got out of there with a good deal of loot and met a man in Julesburg who wanted to come out here. He knew nothing of your crooked background, and. . . ."

Berdue's hand was a streak for his gun, but Haney had expected it. When the Reynolds foreman stepped toward him, he had come beyond Haney's outstretched feet, and Ross whipped his toe up behind the foreman's knee and jerked hard just as he shoved with his open hand. Berdue hit the floor with a crash and his gun went off with a roar, the shot plowing into the ceiling. From the room overhead came an angry shout and the sound of bare feet hitting the floor.

Ross moved swiftly. He stepped over and kicked the gun from Berdue's hand, then swept it up.

"Get up! Reynolds, get over there against the wall, *pronto!*"

White-faced, Reynolds backed to the wall, hatred burning deeply in his eyes. Slowly Sydney Berdue got to his feet, his eyes clinging to his gun in Ross Haney's hand.

"Lift your hands, both of you. Now push them higher. Hold it."

He stared at the two men. Behind him, the room was silent with curious onlookers. "Now," Ross Haney said coolly, "I'm going to finish what I started. You asked me why you deserved to have enemies. I started by telling you about the white people you murdered, and by the guns you sold, and now I'll tell you about the man you met in Julesburg."

Reynolds's face was ashen. "Forget that," he said. "You don't need to talk so much. Berdue was huntin' trouble. You forget it. I need a good man."

"To murder . . . like you did your partner? You made a deal with him, and he came down here and worked hard. He planted those trees. He built that house. Then three of you went out and stumbled into a band of Indians, and somehow, although wounded, you were the only one who got back. And naturally the ranch was all yours. Who were those Indians, Chalk? Or was there only *one* Indian? Only one, who was the last man of three riding single file? You wanted to know why I wouldn't work for you and why you should have enemies. I've told you. And now I'll tell you something more. I've come to the Ruby Hills to stay. I'm not leavin'."

Deliberately he handed the gun back to Berdue, and, as he held it out to him, their eyes met and fastened, and it was Sydney Berdue's eyes that shifted first. He took the gun, reversed it, and started it into his holster, and then his hand stopped and his lips drew tight.

Ross Haney was smiling. "Careful, Berdue," he said softly. "I wouldn't try it, if I were you."

Berdue stared, and then with an oath he shoved the gun hard into its holster and, turning out the door, walked rapidly away. Behind him went Chalk Reynolds, his neck and ears red with the bitterness of the fury that throbbed in his veins.

Slowly, in a babble of talk, Ross Haney seated himself again. "May," he called over to the waitress, "my coffee's cold! Bring me another one, will you?"

Chapter Five

Persons who lived in the town of Soledad were not unaccustomed to sensation, but the calling of Chalk Reynolds and his supposedly gun-slick foreman in the Cattleman's Rest Hotel restaurant was a subject that had the old maids of both sexes licking their lips with anticipation and excitement. Little had been known of the background of Chalk Reynolds. He was the oldest settler, the owner of the biggest and oldest ranch, and he was a hard character when pushed. Yet now they saw him in a new light, and the story went from mouth to mouth.

Not the last to hear it was Walt Pogue, who chuckled and slapped his heavy thigh. "Wouldn't you know it? That old four-flusher! Crooked as a dog's hind leg!"

The next thing that occurred to anyone occurred to him. How did Ross Haney know? The thought brought Pogue to a standstill. Haney knew too much. Who was Haney? If he knew that, he might . . . but, no! That didn't necessarily follow. Still, Ross Haney would be a good friend to have, or a bad enemy.

Not the least of the talk concerned Haney's confidence, the way he had stood there and dared Berdue to draw. Overnight Haney had become the most talked-about man in the Ruby Hills.

When gathering his information about the Ruby Hills country, Ross Haney had gleaned some other information that was of great interest. That information was what occupied his mind on his second day in Soledad.

So far, in his meandering around the country, and he had done more of it than anyone believed, he had had no opportunity to verify this final fragment of information. But now he intended to do it. From what he had overheard, the country north and west of the mountains was a badlands that was avoided by all. It was a lava country, broken and jagged, and there was much evidence of prehistoric volcanic action, so much so that riding there was a danger always, and walking was the surest way to ruin a pair of boots.

Yet at one time there had been a man who knew the lava beds and all of that badlands country that occupied some 300 square miles stretching north and west across the state line. That man had been Jim Burge.

It had been Jim Burge who had told Charlie Hastings, Reynolds's ill-fated partner, about the Ruby Hills country, and it had been Jim Burge who first drove a herd of Spanish cattle into the Ruby Hills. But Burge tired of ranching and headed north, leaving his ranch and turning his horses loose. His cattle were already gone. Gone, that is, into the badlands. Burge knew where they were, but cattle were of no use without a market, and there was no market anywhere near. Burge decided he wanted to move, and he wanted quick money, so he left the country, taking only a few of the best horses with him.

He had talked to Charlie Hastings and Hastings had talked to Chalk Reynolds, but Jim Burge was already gone. Gone east into the Texas Panhandle and a lone-hand fight with Comanches that ended with four warriors dead and with Jim Burge's scalp hanging from the belt of another. But Jim Burge had talked to other people in Santa Fé, and the others did not forget, either. One of these had talked to Ross Haney, and Ross was a curious man.

When he threw his saddle on the Appaloosa, he was planning to satisfy that curiosity. He was going to find out what had become of those cattle. Nine years had passed since Burge left them to shift for themselves. In nine years several hundred cattle can do pretty well for themselves.

"There's water in those badlands if you know where to look," Burge had told the man in Santa Fé, "an' there's grass, but you've got to find it." Knowing range cattle, Ross was not worried about the cattle finding it, and, if they could find it, he would find them—unless someone else had.

So he rode out of Soledad down the main trail, and there were many eyes that followed him out. One pair of these belonged to Sherry Vernon, already out and on her horse, drifting over the range, inspecting her cattle and seeing where they fed. She noted the tall rider on the queerly marked horse, and there was a strange leap in her heart as she watched him heading down the trail.

Was he leaving? For always? The thought gave her a pang, even though, remembering the oddly intent look in his eyes and the hard set to his jaw, she knew he would be back. Of course, she had heard the story of his meeting with Chalk Reynolds and Sydney Berdue. Berdue had always frightened her, for wherever she turned, his eyes were upon her. They gave her a crawling sensation, not at all like the excitement she drew from the quick, amused eyes of Ross Haney.

The Appaloosa was a good mountain horse, and, ears pricked forward, he stepped out eagerly. The sights and smells were what he knew best and he quickened his step, sure he was going home. Ross Haney knew that with his action of the previous day he was in the center of things whether he liked it or not, and he liked it. From now on he would move fast, and with boldness, not too definitely, for it would pay to keep them puzzled for a few days longer. Things would break shortly between Pogue and Reynolds, especially now that his needling of Reynolds would scare the old man into aggressive action.

Chalk was no fool. He would know how fast talk would spread. It might not be long before embarrassing questions might be asked. The only escape from those questions lay in power. He must put himself beyond questions. Eyes squinted against the glare, Haney thought about that, trying to calculate just what Reynolds would do. It was up to him to strike, and he would strike, or Haney knew nothing of men under pressure.

The trail he sought showed itself suddenly, just a faint track off to the right through the piñons, and he took it, letting Río set his own gait. It was mid-afternoon before Ross reached the edge of the lava beds. The black tumbled masses seemed without trails or any sign of vegetation. He skirted the great black, tumbled masses of lava, searching for some evidence of a trail. It was miserably hot, and the sun threw heat back from the blazing rocks until he felt like he was in an oven. When he was on a direct line between the lava beds and Thousand Springs, he rode back up the mountain, halted, and swung down to give his horse a rest.

From his saddlebags he took a telescope, a glass he had bought in New Orleans several years before. Sitting down on a boulder while the Appaloosa cropped casually at the dry grass, he began a systematic, inch by inch study of the lava beds.

Only the vaguest sort of plan had formed in his mind for his next step. Everything had been worked out carefully to this point, but from now on his action depended much upon the actions of Pogue and Reynolds. Yet he did have the vestige of a plan. If the cattle he sought were still in the lava beds, he intended to brand them one by one and shove bunches of them out into the valley. He was going to use that method to make his bid for the valley range.

After a half hour of careful study he got up, thrust the glass in his belt, and rode slowly along the hillside, stopping at intervals to continue his examination of the beds. It was almost dusk when he raised up in the stirrups and pointed the glass toward a tall finger of rock that thrust itself high from the beds. At the base of it was a cow, and it was walking slowly toward the northwest!

Try as he might, Ross could find no trail into the lava beds, so as dusk was near, he turned the Appaloosa and started back toward Thousand Springs. He would try again. At least, he knew he was not shooting in the dark. There was at least one cow in that labyrinth of lava, and, if there was one, there would certainly be more.

The trail he had chosen led him up the mesa at Thousand Springs from a little known route. He wound around through the clumps of piñon until the flat top was reached. Then he rode along slowly, drinking in this beauty that he had chosen for the site of his home. The purple haze had thickened over the hills and darkened among the trees, and deep shadows gathered in the forested notches of the hills while the pines yet made a dark fringe against the sky still red with the last rose of the sinking sun.

Below him, the mesa broke sharply off and fell for over 100 feet of sheer rock. Thirty feet from the bottom of the cliff the springs trickled from the fractured rock and covered the rock below with a silver sheen from many small cascades that fell away into the pool below.

Beyond the far edge of the pool, fringed with aspens, the valley fell away in a long sweep of tall-grass range, rolling into a dark distance against the mystery of the hills. Ross Haney sat his horse in a place rarely seen by man, for he was doubtful if anyone in many years had mounted the mesa. That he was not the first man here, he knew, for there were Indian relics and the remains of stone houses, ages old. These seemed to have no connection with any cliff dwellings or pueblos he had seen in the past. The building was more ancient and more massive than on Acoma, the Sky City.

The range below him was the upper end of Ruby Valley and was supposedly under control of Chalk Reynolds. Actually Reynolds rarely visited the place, nor did his men. It was far away at the end of the range he claimed, and the water was available for the cattle when they wished to come to it. Yet here on the rim of the mesa, or slightly back from the rim, Haney had begun to build a ranch house, using the old foundations of the prehistoric builders, and many of their stones.

The floor itself was intact, and he availed himself of it, sweeping it clean over a wide expanse. He had paced it off, and planned his house accordingly, and he had large ideas. Yet for the moment he was intent only on repairing a part of the house to use as his claim shanty.

There was water here. It bubbled from the same source as that of the Thousand Springs. He knew that his water was the same water. Several times he had tried dropping sticks or leaves into the water outside his door, only to find them later in the pool below.

From where he sat he could with his glass see several miles of trail, and watch all who approached him. The trail up the back way was unknown so far as he could find out. Certainly it indicated no signs of use but that of wild game, although it had evidently been used in bygone years.

To the east and south his view was unobstructed. Below him lay all the dark distance of the valley and the range for which he was fighting. To the north, the mesa broke off sharply and fell away into a deep cañon with a dry wash at its bottom. The side of the cañon across from him was almost as sheer as this and at least a quarter of a mile away.

The trail led up from the west and through a broken country of tumbled rock, long fingers of lava, and clumps of piñon giving way to aspen and pine. The top of the mesa was at least 200 acres in extent and absolutely impossible to reach by any known route but the approach he used.

Returning through the trees to a secluded hollow, Ross swung down and stripped the saddle and bridle from the Appaloosa, then turned it loose. He rarely hobbled or tied the horse, for Río would come at a call or whistle, and never failed to respond at once. But a horse in most cases will not wander far from a campfire, feeding away from it, and then slowly feeding back toward it, seeming to like the feeling of comfort as well as a man did.

He built his fire of dry wood and built it with plenty of cover, keeping it small. Even at this height there was no danger of it being seen and causing wonder. The last thing he wanted now was for any of the people from the valley to find him out.

After he had eaten, he strolled back to the open ground where the house was taking shape. Part of the ancient rock floor he was keeping for a terrace from which the whole valley could be seen.

For a long time he stood there, looking off into the darkness and enjoying the cool night air. Then he turned and walked back into the deep shadows of the house. He was standing there, trying to see it as it would appear when complete when he heard a low, distant rumble.

Suddenly anxious, he listened intently. It seemed to come from within the very rock on which he stood. He waited, listening for the sound to grow. But after a moment it died away to a vague rumble, and then disappeared altogether. Puzzled, he walked around for several minutes, waiting and listening, but there was no further sound.

It was a strange thing, and it disturbed him and left him uneasy as he walked back to his camp. Long after he rolled in his blankets, he lay there puzzling over it. He noted with an odd sense of disquiet that Río stayed close to him, closer than usual. Of course, there could be another reason for that. There were cougars on the mesa and in the breaks behind it. He had seen their tracks. There were also elk and deer, and twice he had seen bear. The country he had chosen was wildly beautiful, a strange, lost corner of the land, somehow cut off from the valley by the rampart of Thousand Springs Mesa.

Ross Haney awakened suddenly as the sky was growing gray, and found himself sitting bolt upright. And then he heard it again, that low, mounting rumble, far down in the rock beneath him, as though the very spirit of the mountain had been rolling over under him in his sleep. Only here the sound was not so plain, it was fainter, farther away.

Chapter Six

At daybreak, Ross rolled out of his blankets, built a fire, and made coffee. While eating, he puzzled over the strange sound he had heard the night before and again before dawn. The only solution that seemed logical was that it came somehow from the springs. It was obvious that forces of some sort were at work deep in the rock of the mesa.

Obviously these forces had made no recent change in the contour of the rock itself, and so must be insufficient for the purpose. Haney continued with his building, working the morning through.

Unlike many cowhands, he had always enjoyed working with his hands. Now he had the pleasure of doing something for himself, with the feeling that he was building to last. By noon he had another wall of heavy stone constructed and the house was beginning to take shape.

He stopped briefly to eat, and slipped on his shirt before sitting down. As he buttoned it up, he saw a faint movement far down the Soledad trail. Going to his saddlebags, he dug out his glass and took his position in a lookout post among the rocks on the rim. First making sure the sunlight would not reflect from the glass and give him away, he dropped flat among the rocks and pointed the glass downtrail.

The rider's face was still indistinct, but there was something vaguely familiar about him. And then, as he drew nearer, Ross saw it was Sydney Berdue.

What was the Reynolds foreman doing here? Of course, as this was considered RR range, he might be checking the grass or the stock. He rode swiftly, however, and paid no attention to anything around him. When he reached the pool below, he swung down, seated himself on a rock, and lighted a cigarette.

Waiting for someone.

The sun felt warm and comfortable on Ross's back after the hard work of the morning and he settled himself comfortably into the warm sand behind the rocks. Thoughtfully he turned his glass down the trail, but saw no one else. Then he began scanning the country and, after a few minutes, picked up another rider. The man rode a sorrel horse with three white stockings and must have approached through the timber as he was not in sight until the last minute. He rode swiftly up to the pool and swung down. The two men shook hands, and, puzzled, Ross shifted his glass to the brand.

The sorrel carried a VV on his shoulder! A Vernon rider at what was apparently a secret meeting with the foreman of the RR! The two seated themselves, and Haney waited, studying them, and then the trail. And now he saw two more horsemen, and these were riding up the trail together. One was a big, slope-shouldered man who he had seen in Soledad, and he rode a Box N horse. The last man rode a gray mustang with the Three Diamonds of Star Levitt on his hip.

Here was something of real interest. The four brands, two of them outwardly at war, the others on the verge of it, meeting in secret. Haney cursed his luck that he could not hear what was said, but so far as he could see, Berdue seemed to be laying down the law.

Then he saw something else.

At first it was a vague suggestion of disturbance in the grass and brush near the foot of the cliff, and then he saw a slight figure, creeping nearer. His heart leaped as he saw Sherry Vernon crawling nearer. Sherry Vernon!

Whatever the meeting of the four men meant, it was at least plain that they intended no one to see or overhear what they had to say. If the girl was seen or heard, she would be in great danger. Sliding back from his lookout point, he hurried in a crouching run toward the house and got his Winchester.

By the time he was back, the brief meeting was breaking up. The girl lay still below him, and the men mounted, one by one, and rode away. The last to go was Sydney Berdue.

After several minutes had passed, Sherry got to her feet and walked out in the open. She went to the spring and drank, then stood looking around, obviously in profound thought.

Ross debated the possibility of getting his horse,

but dismissed it as impossible. It would require a couple of hours at least to ride from here to the spring, although he was within a few hundred feet of it.

The girl walked away toward the woods, finally, evidently going for her horse. After some minutes she rode out of the trees on Flame and started down the trail toward the VV Ranch, distant against the far hills.

There had been a meeting of the four brands, but not of the leaders. Sherry Vernon had probably overheard what was said. He scowled thoughtfully. The girl had moved with care and skill, and her actions showed she was no mean woodsman when it came to playing the Indian. None of the four below had been a tenderfoot, yet she had approached them and listened without giving herself away. Sherry Vernon, he decided, would bear some watching herself.

Saddling Río, Ross rode back through the aspens and down the lonely and dangerous trail to the rim of the badlands. He still had found no way to enter the lava beds, and, if he was to take the next step in his program of conquest, he must find the cattle that he was sure still roamed among those remote and lost water holes in the lava.

The afternoon was well along before he found himself skirting the rim of the cañon that opened near the lava beds, and, when he reached them, it was already late. There would be little time for a search, but, despite that, he turned north, planning to cut back around the mesa and return to Soledad by way of the springs.

A slight movement among the trees ahead

caused him to halt, and then he saw several elk drifting slowly down a narrow glade toward the lava. His eyes narrowed suddenly. There was no water of which he knew closer than the Thousand Springs pool, and these elk were drifting away from it rather than toward it. As they usually watered at sundown or before daybreak, they must be headed for water elsewhere, and that could be in the lava.

Dismounting, he ground-hitched his horse and watched the elk as they drifted along until they had almost vanished in the trees, then he mounted and followed them down. When the trail he was following turned down and joined theirs, he continued along it. In a few minutes he grunted with satisfaction, for the hoof marks led him right up to the lava and into a narrow cleft between two great folds of the black rocks.

Riding carefully, for the trail was very narrow and the lava on both sides black and rough, he kept on, following the elk. It was easy to see how such a trail might exist for years and never be found, for at times he was forced to draw one leg up and lift the stirrup out of the way, as it was too narrow, otherwise.

The trail wound around and around, covering much distance without penetrating very far, and then it dipped down suddenly through a jagged and dangerous-looking cleft. Ross hesitated, studying the loose-hanging crags above with misgiving. They looked too shaky and insecure for comfort. He well knew that if a man was ever trapped or hurt in this lava bed, he might as well give up. There would be no help for him. Yet, with many an upward glance at the great, poorly balanced chunks of rock, many of them weighing many tons, he rode down into the cleft on the trail of the elk.

For over a half mile the cleft led him steadily downward, much of the going very steep, and he realized that he was soon going to be well below the level of the surrounding country. He rode on, however, despite the growing darkness, already great in the dark bottom of the cleft. Then the trail opened out, and he stopped with a gasp of amazement.

Before him lay a great circular valley, an enormous valley surrounded by gigantic black cliffs that in many places shelved out over the edge, but the bottom was almost level and was covered with rich green grass. There were a few scattered clumps of trees, and from somewhere he heard the sound of water.

Drifting on, he looked up and around him, overcome with astonishment. The depth of the valley, at least 1,000 feet lower than the surrounding country, and the unending sameness of the view of the beds from above safely concealed its existence. It was without doubt an ancient volcanic crater, long extinct, and probably the source of the miles of lava beds that had been spewed forth in some bygone age.

The green fields below were dotted with cattle, most of them seemingly in excellent shape. Here and there among them he noticed small groups of horses. Without doubt these were the cattle and horses, or their descendants, left by Jim Burge.

Despite the lateness of the hour, he pushed on, marveling at the mighty walls around him, at the green grass, and the white-trunked aspens. Twice he found springs of water; in both cases they bubbled from the ground. Later, he found one spring that ran from a cleft in the rock and trickled down over the worn face of the cliff for some thirty feet to sink into the ground below. None of the cattle seemed in the least frightened of him, although they moved back as he approached, and several lifted their noses at him curiously.

When he had ridden for well over two miles, he drew up in a small glade near a spring, and, stripping the saddle from his horse, he made camp. This would end his rations, and tomorrow he must start back. Obviously this would be a good place to start such a cache of supplies as Scott had advised.

Night brought a strange coolness to the valley. He built a fire and fixed his coffee, talking to Río meanwhile. After a moment he became conscious of movement. He looked up and saw that a dozen or more cows and a bull had moved up. They were staring at him with their amazed bovine eyes. Apparently they had never seen a man before.

From all appearances, the crater was a large one, being several miles across and carpeted with this rich grass. The cattle were all in good shape. Twice during the night he heard the cry of a cougar and once the howl of a wolf.

With daylight he was in saddle once more, but by day the crater proved to be smaller than he had at first believed, and there was probably some 2,000 acres in the bottom. But it was all the same level ground with rich grass and a good bit of timber, all things considered.

Twice, when skirting the edges of the crater, he found ice caves. These he knew were caused by the mass cooling so unevenly that, when the surface had become cold and hard, the material below was still molten. As the fluid drained away, caves were formed under the solid crust. Because lava is a poor heat conductor, the cold air of the caves was protected. Ice formed there, and no matter how warm it might be on the surface, there was always snow in the caves. At places pools of clear, cold water had formed. He could see that some of these had been used as watering places by the deer, elk, and wild horses.

When at last he started back toward the cleft through which he had gained entrance to the crater, he was sure there were several hundred, perhaps as many as 600 head of wild cattle in the bottom of the crater.

He rode out, but not with any feeling of comfort. Someday he would scale those cliffs and have a look at the craggy boulders on the rim. If someone ever fell into the cleft, whoever or whatever was in the bottom would never come out.

It was dusk of another evening before the Appaloosa cantered down the one street of Soledad and drew up at the livery stable. A Mexican came to the door, glanced at him, and then accepted his horse. He looked doubtfully at the strange brand.

"You ride for *Señor* Pogue or *Señor* Reynolds?" he asked hesitantly.

"For myself," Ross said. "What's the matter? The town seems quiet."

"*Sí, señor*. There has been a keeling. Rolly Burt of

the RR was in a shooting with two hands from the Box N. One of them was killed, the other wounded, and *Señor* Burt has disappeared."

"Left the country?"

"Who knows? He was wounded, they say, and I am sorry for that. He was a good man, *Señor* Burt." The Mexican lighted a smoke, glancing at Haney. "Perhaps he was no longer wanted on the RR, either."

"Why do you say that?" Ross asked quickly. "Have you any reason for it?"

"*Sí.* He has told me himself that he has trouble weeth *Señor* Berdue."

Berdue had trouble with Burt, yet Burt was attacked by two Box N hands? That didn't seem to tie in, or did it? Could there be any connection between this shooting and the meeting at the springs? In any event, this would probably serve to start hostilities again.

Chapter Seven

Leaving his horse to be cared for, Ross returned to his room in the Cattleman's Rest Hotel. Kinney was not in the lobby when he crossed it, and he found no one on the stairs. He knew how precarious was his own position, for while the house he was building was reasonably safe from discovery, there was no reason to believe that someone would not soon discover the ground had been plowed back under the trees. It wasn't much, but enough to indicate he was working on the place.

Uneasily he surveyed the situation. So far everything was proceeding according to plan, and almost too well. He had his water rights under control. He had found the cattle. He had in the crater and on the mesa two bases of action that were reasonably safe from attack, yet the situation was due to blow up at almost any moment.

Berdue seemed to be playing a deep game. It might be with the connivance of his uncle, but he might be on his own. Perhaps someone else had the same idea he had, that from the fighting of Pogue and Reynolds would come a new system of things in the Ruby Hills country. Perhaps Berdue, or some other unnamed person or group, planned to be top dog.

Berdue's part in it puzzled Haney, but at least he knew by sight the men Berdue had met secretly and would be able to keep a closer watch on them. Also, there were still the strange hardcases who lived and worked on the VV. Somehow they did not seem to fit with what he had seen of the Vernons. *The next order of business,* he told himself, *is a visit to the VV.*

A dozen people were eating in the hotel restaurant when he entered. He stopped at one side of the door and surveyed the groups with care. It would not do to walk into Berdue or Reynolds unawares, for Berdue would not, and Reynolds dared not, ignore him. He had stepped into the scene in Soledad in no uncertain terms.

Suddenly, at a small table alone, he saw Sherry Vernon. On an impulse, he walked over to her, his spurs jingling. She glanced up at him, momentarily surprised.

"Oh, it's you again? I thought you had left town."

"You know better than that." He indicated the chair opposite her. "May I sit down?"

"Surely." She looked at him thoughtfully. "You know, Ross Haney, you're not an entirely unhandsome sort of man, but I've a feeling you're still pretty savage."

"I live in a country that is savage," he said simply. "It is a country that is untamed. The last court of appeal is a six-shooter."

"From all I hear, you gave Sydney Berdue some uncomfortable moments without one. You're quite an unusual man. Sometimes your language sounds like any cowboy, and sometimes it doesn't, and sometimes your ideas are different."

"You find men of all kinds in the West. The town drunk in Julesburg, when I was there, could quote Shakespeare and had two degrees. I punched cows on the range in Texas with the brother of an English lord."

"Are you suggesting that you are a duke in disguise?"

"Me?" He grinned. "No, I'm pretty much what I seem. I'm a cowhand, a drifter. Only I've got a few ideas and I've read a few books. I spent a winter once snowed up in the mountains in Montana with two other cowhands. All we had for entertainment was a couple of decks of cards, some checkers, and a half dozen books. Some Englishman left them there, and I expect before spring we all knew those books by heart, an' we'd argued every point in them."

"What were they?" she asked curiously.

"Plutarch's *Lives*, the plays and sonnets of Shakespeare, some history . . . oh, a lot of stuff. And good reading. We had a lot of fun with those books. When we'd played cards and checkers until we were black in the face, we'd ask each other questions on the books, for by the time we'd been there half the winter we'd read them several times over."

He ate in silence for a few minutes, and then she asked: "Do you know anything about the shooting?"

"Heard about it. What sort of man is Rolly Burt?"

"One of the best. You'd like him, I think. Hard as nails, and no youngster. He's more than forty, I'd say. But he says what he thinks, and he thinks a good deal."

Ross hesitated a few minutes, and then said: "By the way, I saw one of your hands in town yesterday. A tall, slope-shouldered fellow in a checkered shirt. You know the one I mean?"

She looked up at him, her eyes cool and direct. He had an uncomfortable feeling that she knew more than she was allowing him to think she did. Of course, this was the man she had watched from hiding as he met Berdue. Probably she had overheard their talk.

"Oh, you mean Kerb Dahl! Yes, he's one of our hands. Why do you ask?"

"Wondering about him. I'm trying to get folks placed around here."

"There are a lot of them trying to get you placed, too."

He laughed. "Sure! I expected that. Are you one of them?"

"Yes, I think I am. You remember I overheard your talk on the trail and I'm still wondering where you plan to be top dog?"

He flushed. "You shouldn't have heard that. However, I back down on none of it. I know how Chalk Reynolds got his ranch. I know how Walt Pogue got his, and neither of them has any moral nor other claim to them aside from possession, if that is a right. You probably heard what I told Chalk in here the other day. I could tell him more. I haven't started on Pogue yet, and I'd as soon you didn't tell anyone I plan to. However, in good time I shall. You see, he ran old man Carter off his place, and he had Emmett Chubb kill Vin Carter. That's one of the things that drew me here."

"Revenge?"

"Call it what you like. I have a different name for it." He leaned toward her, suddenly eager for her to understand. "You see, you can't judge the West by any ordered land you know. It is a wild, hard land, and the men that came West and survived were tough stern men. They fought Indians and white men who were worse than Indians. They fought winter, flood, storm, drought, and starvation. There's a sheriff here in town who was practically appointed by Chalk Reynolds. The jail here stands on Reynolds's land. The nearest court is over two hundred miles away, over poor roads and through Indian country. North of us there is one of the wildest and most remote lands in North America where a criminal could escape and hide for years. The only law we have here is the law of strength. The only justice we have must live in the hearts and minds of men. The land is hard, and so the men are hard. We make mistakes, of course, but when there is a case of murder, we try to handle the murderer so he will not kill again. Someday we will have law. We will have order. Then we can let the courts decide, but now we have none of those things. If we find a mad dog, we kill him, for there is no dogcatcher or law to do it. If we find a man who kills unfairly, we punish him. If two men fight and all is equal, regardless of which cause is right, we let the killing stand. But if a man is shot in the back, without a gun or a fair chance, then the people or sometimes one man must act.

"I agree that it is not right. I agree that it should be different, but this is yet a raw, hard land, and we must have our killers, not punished, but prevented from killing again. Vin Carter was my friend. Of that I can say nothing, only that because he was my friend, I must act for him. He was not a gunfighter. He was a brave young man, a fair shot, and, on the night he was killed, he was so drunk he could scarcely see. He did not even know what was happening. It was murder.

"So I have come here. It so happens that I am like some of these men. Perhaps I am ruthless. Perhaps in the long run I shall lose, and perhaps I shall gain. No man is perfect. No man is altogether right or altogether wrong. Pogue and Reynolds got their ranches and power through violence. They are now in a dog-eat-dog feud of their own. When that war is over, I expect to have a good ranch. If it leaves them both alive and in power, I shall have my ranch, anyway."

She looked at him thoughtfully. "Where, Ross?"

His pulse leaped at the use of his first name, and he smiled suddenly. "Does it matter now? Let's wait, and then I'll tell you." The smile left his face. "By the way, as you left me the other day, a man told me you were a staked claim, and to stay away."

"What did you do?" She looked at him gravely, curiously.

"I told him he was a fool to believe any woman was a staked claim unless she wanted it so. And he said, nevertheless you were staked. If it is of interest, you might as well know that I don't believe him. Also, I wouldn't pay any attention if I did."

She smiled. "I would be surprised if you did. Nevertheless"—her chin lifted a little—"what he said is true."

Ross Haney's heart seemed to stop. For a full minute he stared at her, amazed and wordless. Then he said: "You mean . . . what?"

"I mean that I'm engaged to marry Star Levitt. I have been engaged to him for three months." She arose swiftly. "I must be going now." Her hand dropped suddenly to his with a gentle pressure, and then she was gone.

He stared after her. His thoughts refused to order themselves, for of all the things she might have said, or that he might have expected, this was the last. Sherry Vernon was engaged to Star Levitt.

"Some hot coffee?" It was May, smiling down at him.

"Sure." She cleaned up the table, then left him alone. *Sure,* he mused, *that's the way it would be. I meet a girl worth having and she belongs to somebody else!*

"Mind if I sit down?"

He looked up to see Allan Kinney, the hotel clerk, standing by the table. "Go ahead," he suggested, "and have some coffee."

May delivered the coffee, and for a few moments there was silence.

"Ross, you'd do a lot for a friend, wouldn't you?"

Surprised, he glanced up and something in Kinney's eyes told him what was coming. "Why, sure!" But even as he said it, he was thinking it over, thinking over what he knew Kinney had on his mind.

"Do you regard me as a friend? Of course, I haven't known you long, but you seem like a regular fellow. You haven't any local ties that I can see."

"That's right! I just cut the last one. Or had it cut. What do you want me to do? Get him out of town?"

Kinney jerked up sharply. "You mean . . . you know?"

"I guessed. Where else would he go? Is Burt hurt bad?"

"He can ride. He's a good man, Ross. One of the best. I had no idea what to do about him because I know they will think of the hotel soon."

"You've got him here?" Haney was incredulous. "We'd best get him out tonight. That Box N crowd will be in hunting for him, and I've got a hunch the RR outfit won't back him the least bit."

"He's in the potato cellar. In a box under the potatoes."

"Whatever made you ask me?" Ross demanded.

Kinney shrugged. "Well, like I said, you hadn't any ties here, and seemed on the prod, as they say in Soledad. Then, May suggested it. May did, and Sherry."

"She knows?"

"I thought of her first. The VV is out of this fight so far, and it seemed the only place. She told me she would like to, but there were reasons why it was the very worst place for him. Then she suggested you."

"She did?"

"Uhn-huh. She said, if you liked Burt, she knew you would do it, and you might do it just as a slap at Reynolds and Pogue. She didn't seem to believe Reynolds would help, either."

Haney digested this thoughtfully. Apparently Sherry had a pretty good idea of just what undercurrents were moving the pawns about in the Soledad chess game. Of course, she would have heard at least part of Berdue's talk with Kerb Dahl and the others.

"We can't wait," Haney said. "It will have to be done now. The Box N hands should be getting to town within the hour. Have you got a spare horse?"

"Not that we can get without everybody knowing, but May has one at her place," Kinney answered. "She lives on the edge of town. The problem is to get him there."

"I'll get him there," Haney promised. "But I'd best get mounted myself. I know where to take him, too. However, you'd best throw us together a sack of grub from the restaurant supplies so there won't be too many questions asked. After I come back again, I can arrange to get some stuff."

Ross Haney got to his feet. "Get him ready to move. I'll get my horse down to May's and come back." He listened while Kinney gave him directions about finding her house, and then hurried to the door.

It was too late.

A dozen hard-riding horsemen came charging up the street and they swung down at the hotel. One man stepped up on the boardwalk and strode into the hotel. Haney knew him by his size. It was Walt Pogue himself, and the man at his right was the man who had been with Berdue at the springs!

"Kinney! I want to search your place! That killer Rolly Burt is somewhere in town, an' by the Lord Harry we'll have him hangin' from a cottonwood limb before midnight!"

"What makes you think he'd be here?" Kinney demanded. He was pale and taut, but completely self-possessed. He might have been addressing a class in history, or reading a paper before a literary group. "I know Burt, but I haven't seen him."

Chapter Eight

Unobtrusively Ross Haney was lounging against the door to the kitchen, his mind working swiftly. They would find Burt, and there was no earthly way to prevent it. The only chance would be to avert the hanging, to delay it. He knew suddenly that he was not going to see Rolly Burt hang. He didn't know the man, but Burt had won his sympathy by winning a fair fight against two men.

"What are you so all fired wrought up about, Pogue?" he drawled.

Walt Pogue turned squarely around to face him. "It's you! What part have you got in this?"

Ross shrugged. "None at all. Just wonderin'. Everywhere I been, if a man is attacked an' kills two men against his one, he's figured to be quite a man, not a lynchin' job."

"He killed a Box N man!"

"Sure." Ross smiled. "Box N men can die as well as any others. It was a fair shake from all I hear. All three had guns, all three did some shootin'. I haven't heard any Reynolds men kickin' because it was two against one. Kind of curious, that. I'm wonderin' why all the RR men are suddenly out of town?"

"You wonder too much!" It was the man from the springs. "This is none of your deal! Keep out of it!"

Ross Haney still leaned against the door, but his eyes turned to the man from the springs. Slowly, carefully, contemptuously he looked the rider over from head to heel, then back again. Then he said softly: "Pogue, you've got a taste for knick-knacks. If you want to take this boy home with you, keep him out of trouble."

The rider took a quick step forward. "You're not running any bluff on me, Haney!"

"Forget it, Voyle! You get to huntin' for Burt. I'll talk to Haney." Pogue's voice was curt.

Voyle hesitated, his right hand hovering over his gun, but Ross did not move, lounging carelessly against the doorpost, a queer half smile on his face.

With an abrupt movement then, Voyle turned away, speaking quickly over his shoulder. "We'll talk about it later, Haney!"

"Sure," Ross Haney said, and then as a parting he called softly: "Want to bring Dahl with you?"

Voyle caught himself in mid-stride, and Voyle's shoulders hunched as if against a blow. He stopped and stared back, shock, confusion, and puzzlement struggling for expression.

Haney looked back at Pogue. "You carry some characters," he said. "That Voyle now. He's touchy, ain't he?"

"What did you mean about Dahl? He's not one of my riders!"

"Is that right? I thought maybe he was, although I'll admit I didn't know."

Walt Pogue stared at him, annoyed and angry, yet puzzled, too. The big man walked back to the restaurant stove, got a cup, and poured coffee into it from the big coffee pot. He put sugar in it, and then cream. He glanced over his shoulder at Ross.

Haney felt a slight touch on his shoulder and glanced around and found May at his shoulder.

"He's gone!" she whispered. "He's not there."

There was dust on her dress and he slapped at it, and she hurriedly brushed it away. "Where was he shot?" he asked, under his breath.

"In the leg. He couldn't go far, I know."

Pogue turned around. "What are you two talking about?" he demanded. "Why the whispering?"

"Is it any of your business?" Haney said sharply.

Walt Pogue stiffened and put his cup down hard. "You'll go too far, Haney! Don't try getting rough with me! I won't take it!"

"I'm not askin' you to," Ross replied roughly. He straightened away from the doorpost. "I don't care how you take it. You're not running me or any part of me, and you might as well learn that right now. If I choose to whisper to a girl, I'm doin' it on my own time, so keep out of it."

Pogue stared at him, and then at the girl, and there was meanness in his eyes. He shrugged. "It's a small matter. With all this trouble I'm gettin' jumpy."

Voyle came back into the room accompanied by two other men. "No sign of him, boss. We've been all over the hotel. Simmons an' Clatt went through the vegetable cellar, too, but there ain't a sign of him. There was an empty box under those spuds, though, big enough to hide a man."

Allan Kinney had come back into the room.

"What about that, Kinney?" Pogue demanded.

"Probably somethin' to keep the spuds off the damp ground, much as possible," Haney suggested carelessly. "Seems simple enough."

Pogue's jaw set and he turned swiftly. "You, Haney! Keep out of this! I was askin' Kinney, not you!"

This time Voyle had nothing to say. Ross glanced at him, and the man looked hastily away. *He's scared*, Ross told himself mentally. *He's mixed in some deal and doesn't want his boys to know it. He's afraid I'll say too much.*

Pogue turned and strode from the restaurant, going out through the hotel lobby, his men trooping after him. When the last man was gone, May turned to Kinney. "Allan, where can he be? He was there, you know he was there!"

Kinney nodded. "I know." He twisted his hands together. "He must have heard them and got out somehow. But where could he go?"

Ross Haney was already far ahead of them. He was thinking rapidly. The searchers would probably stop for a drink, but they would not stop long. Voyle was apparently in on the plot to have Burt killed, for he had been at the springs, and this had happened too swiftly. Too little noise had come from the RR for it to be anything but a plot among them. Or so it seemed to Haney. For some reason Rolly Burt had become dangerous to them, and he was supposed to die in the gunfight the previous night, but had survived and killed one of their men and wounded another. Now he must be killed, and soon.

Yet Haney was thinking further than that. His mind was going outside into the darkness, thinking of where he would go if he were a wounded man with little ammunition and no time to get away. He would have to hobble or to drag himself. He would be quickly noticed by anyone and quickly investigated. He would not dare go too far without shelter, for there was some light outside even though it was night.

Then Haney was recalling the stone wall. It started not far from the hotel stables and went around an orchard planted long ago. Some of the stones had fallen, but much of it was intact. A man might make a fair defense from behind that wall, and he could drag himself all of a hundred yards behind it.

Ross walked swiftly out of the hotel through the back door. There in the darkness he stood stockstill at the side of the door, letting his eyes become accustomed to the night. After a minute or two he could pick out the stable, the orchard, and the white of the stones in the wall.

Walking to the stable, he took the path along the side, then put a hand on the stone wall, and dropped over it with a quick vault. Then he stood still once more. If he approached Burt too suddenly, the wounded man might mistake him for an enemy and shoot. Nor did he know Burt, or Burt him.

Moving silently, Haney worked his way along the stone wall. It was no more than three feet high and along much of it there was a hedge of weeds and brambles. He ripped a scratch on his hand, then swore. Softly he moved ahead, and he was almost to the corner when a voice spoke, very low.

"All right, mister, you've made a good guess but a bad one. Let one peep out of you an' you can die."

"Burt?"

"Naw!" the cowhand was disgusted. "This is King Solomon an' I'm huntin' the Queen of Sheba! Who did you think it would be?"

"Listen, an' get this straight the first time. I'm your friend, and a friend of May's and Kinney's from the hotel. I've been huntin' you to help you out of here. There's a horse at May's shack, an' we've got to get you there just as fast as we can make it. You hear?"

"How do I know who you are?"

"I'd have yelled, wouldn't I? If I found you?"

"Oncet, maybe. No more than oncet, though. This Colt still carries a kick. Who are you? I can't see your face."

"I'm Ross Haney. Just blew in."

"The *hombre* that backed down Syd Berdue? Sure thing. I know you. Heard all about it. It was a good job."

"Can you walk?"

"I can take a stab at it if you give me a shoulder."

"Let's go then."

With an arm around Burt's waist, Haney got him over the fence and then down the dark alleyway between it and the stone house next to it. They came out in an open space, and beyond it there was the trail, and then the woods. Once in the shelter of the trees they would have ample concealment all the way to May's house.

Yet once they were started across that open space, any door opened along the backs of the buildings facing them from across the street would reveal them and they would be caught in the open. There would be nothing for it then but to shoot it out.

"All right, Burt. Here we go! If any door opens, freeze where you are!"

"Where you takin' me?" Supporting himself with a hand on Haney's shoulder, and Haney's arm around his waist, he made a fair shift at hobbling along.

"May's shack. If anything delays me, get there. Take her horse an' light out. You know that old trail to the badlands?"

"Sure, but it ain't no good unless you circle around to Thousand Springs. No water. An' that's one mighty rough ride."

"Don't worry. I'll handle that. You get over there and find a spot to watch the trail until you see me. But with luck we'll make it together."

Burt's grip on Haney's shoulder tightened. "Watch it! Somebody openin' that door."

They stopped, standing stockstill. Ross felt Burt's off arm moving carefully, and then he saw the cowhand had drawn a gun. He was holding it across his stomach, covering the man who stood in the light of the open door. It was a saloon bartender.

Somebody loomed over the fat bartender's shoulder. "Hey! Who's that out there?"

"Go on back to your drinks," the bartender said. "I'll go see." He came down the steps and stalked out toward them, and Haney slid his hand down for his left gun.

The fat man walked steadily toward them until he was close by. He glanced from one face to the other. "Pat," Burt said softly, "you'd make a soft bunk for this lead."

"Don't fret yourself," he said. "If I hadn't come, one of those drunken Box N riders would have, an' then what? You shoot me, an' you have them all out here. Go on, beat it. I'm not huntin' trouble with any side." He looked at Haney. "Nor with you, Ross. You don't remember me, but I remember you right well from your fuss with King Fisher. Get goin' now."

He turned and strode back to the door.

"What is it?" A drunken voice called. "If it's Rolly Burt, I'll fix him!"

"It ain't. Just a Mex kid with a horse. Some stray he picked up, an old crow-bait. Forget it!"

The door closed.

Ross heaved a sigh. Without further talk, they moved on, hobbling across the open, then into the trees. There they rested. They heard a door slam open. Men came out into the street and started up the path away from them. They had been drinking and were angry. The town of Soledad would be an unpleasant place on this night.

When Haney had the mare saddled, he helped Rolly up. "Start down the trail," he said. "If you hear anybody comin', get out of sight. When I come, I'll be ridin' that Appaloosa of mine. You've seen it?"

"Sure. I'll know it. I keep goin' until you catch up, right?"

"Right. Keep out of sight of anybody else, and I

mean *anybody*. That goes for your RR hands as well. Hear me?"

"Yeah, an' I guess you're right at that. They sure haven't been much help. But I'll not forget what you've done, a stranger, too."

"You ride. Forget about me. I've got to get back into Soledad an' get my horse out without excitin' comment. Once I get you where I'm takin' you, nobody will find you."

He watched the mare start up the road at a fast walk, and then he turned back toward the town.

He heard shouts and yells, and then a drunken cowhand blasted three shots into the air.

Ross Haney hitched his guns into place and started down the road into Soledad. He was walking fast.

Chapter Nine

The disappearance of Rolly Burt was a nine-day wonder in the town of Soledad and the Ruby Hills. Ross Haney, riding in and out of town, heard the question discussed and argued from every standpoint. Burt had not been seen in Rico, nor in Pie Town. Nor had any evidence of him been found on the trails. No horses were accounted missing, and the search of the Box N cowhands had been fruitless. Neither Allan Kinney nor May asked any questions of Ross, although several times he recognized their curiosity.

The shooting and the frenzied search that followed had left the town abnormally quiet. Yet the rumor was going around that with the end of the coming roundup, the whole trouble would break open again and be settled, once and for all. For the time being, with the roundup in the offing, both ranches seemed disposed to ignore the feud and settle first things first.

Second only to the disappearance of Rolly Burt

was Ross Haney himself as a topic of conversation. He spent money occasionally, and he came and went around Soledad, but no one seemed to have any idea what he was doing, or what his plans were. Curiosity was growing, and the three most curious men were Walt Pogue, Chalk Reynolds, and Star Levitt. There was another man even more curious, and that one was Emmett Chubb.

It was after the disappearance of Burt that Chubb first heard of Haney's presence in the Ruby Hills. The RR hands ate at one long table presided over by Chalk himself, and Syd Berdue sat always at his right hand.

"Heard Walt Pogue an' his man Voyle had some words with that Haney," Reynolds said to Berdue. "Looks like he's gettin' this country buffaloed."

Berdue went white to the lips and started to make an angry reply when he was cut off by the sudden movement down the table. Emmett Chubb had lunged to his feet. The stocky, hard-faced gunman leaned across the table. "Did you say Haney?" he rasped. "Would that be Ross Haney?"

"That's right." Reynolds looked up sharply. "Know him?"

Chubb sat back in his chair with a thud. "I should smile I know him. He's a-huntin' me."

"You?" Reynolds stared. "Why?"

Chubb shrugged. "Me an' a friend of his had a run-in. You knew him. Vin Carter."

"Ah? Carter was a friend of Haney's?" Reynolds chewed in silence. "How good is this Haney?"

"He thinks he's plumb salty. I wouldn't be for knowin', however. Down thataway they sure set store by him."

A slim, dark-faced cowhand looked up and drawled softly: "I know him, Emmett, an', when you tangle with him, be ready. He's the *hombre* who went into King Fisher's hide-out in Mexico after a horse one of Fisher's boys stole off him. He rode the horse out, too, an' the story is that he made Fisher take water. He killed the *hombre* who stole his horse. The fellow was a fool half-breed who went for his gun."

"So he's chasin' you, Emmett?" Reynolds muttered. "Maybe that accounts for his bein' here."

"An' maybe he's here because of Vin Carter," Berdue said. "If he is, that spells trouble for Pogue. That won't hurt us any."

In the days that had followed the escape of Rolly Burt, Haney had not been idle. He had thrown and branded several of the wild cattle, and had pushed a few of them out into the open valley below Thousand Springs. There would be plenty of time later to bring more of them; all he wanted was for the brand to show up when the roundup was under way.

Astride the Appaloosa, he headed for the VV. The morning was warm, but pleasant, and he rode down into the shade under the giant old cottonwoods feeling very fit and very happy. Several of the hands were in sight, and one of them was the slope-shouldered Dahl, mending a saddle girth.

Bob Vernon saw him and his brow puckered in a slight frown. He turned and walked toward Ross Haney. "Get down, won't you? Sherry has been telling me something about you."

"Thanks, I will. Is she here?" His purpose had been to verify, if he could, some of his ideas about that conversation he had seen and she had overheard at the springs. Also, he was curious about the set-up at the VV. It was the one place he had not catalogued in his long rides.

"Yes," Vernon hesitated, "she's here." He made no move to get her. Suddenly he seemed to make a decision. "I say, Haney. You're not coming with the idea of courting my sister, are you? You know she's spoken for."

"That idea," Haney said grimly, "seems to be one everyone wants to sell me. First heard it from Star Levitt."

Vernon's lips tightened. "You mean Star talked to you about Sherry?"

"He did. And Sherry told me she was to marry him."

Bob Vernon appeared relieved. He relaxed. "Well, then you understand how things are. I wouldn't want any trouble over her. Star's pretty touchy."

"Understand this." Haney turned sharply around and faced Bob. "I was told that by Levitt and by Sherry. Frankly the fact that she is engaged to him doesn't make a lot of difference to me. I haven't told that to her, but you're her brother, and I'm tellin' you. You don't need any long-winded explanations about how I feel about her. When I'm sure she's in love with him, I'll keep away. Until then, I'm in to stay."

Surprisingly Vernon did not get angry. He appeared more frightened and worried. "I was afraid of that," he muttered. "I should have known."

"Now, if you won't get her for me, I'll go to the house after her."

"After whom?" They turned swiftly to see Sherry walking toward them, smiling. "Hello, Ross. Who were you coming after? Who could ever make your voice sound like that?"

"You," he said bluntly. "Nobody but you."

Her smile vanished, but there was warmth in her eyes. "That's nice," she said. "You say it as if you mean it."

"I do."

"Boss?" A tall, lean, and red-headed cowhand had walked up to them, and, when they turned, he asked: "Who has the Gallows Frame brand?"

"Gallows Frame?" Vernon shrugged. "Never heard of it. Where did you see it?"

"Up toward Thousand Springs. Seen several mighty fine-lookin' bulls an' a few cows up thataway an' all wearin' that brand, a gallows frame with a ready noose hangin' from it. An' them cows, why they are wilder'n all get out. Couldn't get anywhere near 'em."

"That's something new," Vernon commented. "Have you seen any of them, Sherry?"

She shook her head, but there was a strange expression in her eyes. She glanced over at Ross Haney, who listened with an innocence combined with humor that would have been a perfect giveaway to anyone who knew him.

"No, I haven't seen any of them, Bob." She looked at the redhead again. "Mabry, have you met Ross Haney? He's new around here, but I imagine he's interested in brands."

Mabry turned to Haney and grinned. "Heard somethin' about you," he said. "Seems you had a run-in with Syd Berdue."

Ross noted that Kerb Dahl's fingers had almost ceased to move in their work on the girth.

Mabry walked away with Bob Vernon, and Sherry turned to Ross, her eyes cool but friendly. "I thought you might be interested in knowing Bill Mabry. He was always a good friend of that cowhand they were looking for in town . . . Rolly Burt."

Haney's eyes shifted to her thoughtfully. There seemed to be very little this girl did not know. She would be good to have for a friend, and not at all good as an enemy. She was as intelligent as she was beautiful. Her eyes never seemed asleep, for she seemed to see everything and to comprehend what she was seeing. Was that a lucky guess about Burt? Or did she know? Would Kinney have told her?

Of course, he recalled, Kinney had said she had suggested him. That might be it. She was guessing.

Dahl's ears were obviously tuned to catch every word, so he turned. "Shall we walk over and sit down?" He took her elbow and guided her to a seat under one of the huge cottonwoods.

"Sherry," he said suddenly, "I told Bob I didn't intend to pay no attention to this engagement of yours unless I found out you were in love with Levitt. Are you?"

She looked away quickly, her face suddenly pale and her lips tight. Finally she spoke. "Why else would a girl be engaged to a man?"

"I haven't any idea. There might be reasons." He stared at her, and then his eyes strayed to Dahl. "Until you tell me you do, and look me in the eye when you say it, I'm goin' ahead. I want you, Sherry. I want you like I never wanted anything in this world, an' I mean to have you if you could care for me. I'm not askin' you now. Just tellin' you. When I came into this valley, I came expectin' trouble, an' I thought I knew all the angles. Well, I've found out there's somethin' more goin' on here than I expected, an' it's somethin' you know about.

"Maybe you don't know it all. I'm bankin' you don't. You heard me talkin' to myself. Well, what I said then goes. I'm here alone, an' I'm ridin' for my own brand, an' you've guessed right, for that Gallows Frame is mine, an' the noose is for anybody who wants to hang on it. The RR spread an' the Box N are controlled by a couple of range pirates. They whipped and murdered smaller, weaker men to get what they've got. If they keep it, they'll know they've been in a fight."

Sherry had listened intently. Her face had become serious. "You can't do anything alone, Ross. You must have help." She put her hand on his arm. "Ross, is Rolly safe? Understand, I am not asking you where he is, just if he is safe. He did me a good turn once, and he's an honest man."

"He's safe. For your own information, and not to be repeated, he's workin' for me now. But he can't do much for another ten days or more, an' by that time it may be too late. Can I rely on Mabry?"

"You can. If he will work for you, he will die for you, and kill for you if it's in the right kind of fight. He was Burt's best friend."

"Then, if I can talk to him, you'll lose a hand." He looked down at her. "Sherry, what's goin' on here? Who is Star Levitt? Who are those men I saw in town? This Kerb Dahl here, and Voyle? I know there's some connection."

She got up quickly. "I can't talk about that. Star Levitt is going to be my husband."

Ross got up, too. Roughly he picked up his hat and jerked it on his head, then stood there, hands on hips, staring at her.

"Not Levitt!" he said harshly. "Well, if you won't tell me, I'll find out, anyway."

He turned abruptly, and saw the two men he had seen in town at the restaurant—Kerb Dahl and the shorter, hard-faced man.

In that single instant he became aware of many things. Bob Vernon stood in the door, white as death. Kerb Dahl, a hard gleam in his eyes, was on the right and he walked with elbows bent, hands swinging at his gun butts. Behind them Haney could see the big, old tree with a bench around it, and a rusty horseshoe nailed to the trunk. Two saddled horses stood near the corral, and the sunlight through the leaves dappled the earth with shadow.

Behind him there was a low moan of fear from Sherry, but he did not move, only waited and watched the two men coming toward him. It could be here. It could be now. It could be at this moment.

Dahl spoke first, his lean, cadaverous face hard and with a curiously set expression. The shorter man had moved apart from him a little. Haney remembered the girl behind him, and knew he dare not fight—but some sixth sense warned him that somewhere else would be a third man, probably with a rifle. The difference.

Kerb Dahl spoke. "You're Ross Haney. I reckon you know me. I'm Dahl, an' this here is the first time you've come to the VV, an' this is goin' to be the last. You come on this place again an' you get killed. We don't aim to have no troublemakers around."

Ross Haney held very still, weighing his next words carefully. This could break into a shooting match in one instant. "Then have your artillery ready when I come back," he warned them. "Because, when I'm ready, I'll come back."

"We told you."

Ross looked them over coldly, knowing they had expected to find him as tough and ready for a fight as he had been with Chalk Reynolds and Berdue. Yet there was a queer sense of relief in their eyes, too. Haney guessed that, while there must be a hidden rifleman, these men were afraid for their skins.

Mabry stood nearby as Ross swung into the saddle. "I've got a job for you if you can get to town within the next twelve hours. At the saloon. You might run into a friend of yours."

Mabry did not reply, so Haney rode away, leaving the cowhand standing there. He had spoken softly enough so he knew he was not overheard. Yet Haney knew he was no closer to a solution than before.

There was danger here. An odd situation existed in the Ruby Hills. Scowling, he considered it. On the one hand was Walt Pogue with Bob Streeter and Repp Hanson, two notorious killers. On the other was Chalk Reynolds with Syd Berdue and Emmett Chubb.

Here at the VV was a stranger situation. Bob and Sherry Vernon, who owned the ranch, seemed completely dominated by Levitt and their own hands. Also Levitt had a strong claim of some kind on Sherry herself. What could be behind that? Scowling, Ross considered it. Whatever it was, it could mean everything to him, not only for his plans in the valley, but because of his love for Sherry.

Somewhere in this patchwork of conflicting interests, there was another grouping, that small band that had gathered at the springs with Syd Berdue. The band was made up of at least one man from each ranch—of Kerb Dahl of the VV, Voyle of the Box N, and Tolman of the Three Diamonds.

Where did this last group stand? Voyle, from his actions, wanted Pogue to know nothing of his tie-up with Dahl. Did Reynolds know about Burdue's meeting at the springs? Who was behind it?

Chapter Ten

Quiet reigned at the Bit and Bridle when Ross Haney rode into town in the late afternoon. He left his horse at the rail and strolled through the half doors to the cool interior.

Only Pat, the bartender, was present. The room was dusky and still. Pat idly polished glasses as he came in, glanced up at him, and then put a bottle and a glass on the bar. Ross leaned an elbow on the hardwood and dug out the makings. He built a smoke without speaking, liking the restfulness and coolness after his hot ride, and thinking over what he had seen at the VV.

"You've lived here a long time, Pat?"

"Uhn-huh. Before Carter was killed."

"Lots of changes?"

"Lots."

"There's goin' to be more, Pat."

"Room for 'em."

"Where do you stand?"

Pat turned sharply and fixed his eyes on Haney.

"Not in the middle. Not with Reynolds or Pogue. As for you, I'm neither for you nor against you."

"That's plain enough." Haney didn't know whether to be pleased or angry. After Pat's attitude in regard to Burt, he had hoped he might be an ally. "But you don't sound like much help."

"That's right. No help at all. I've got my saloon. I'm doin' all right. I was here before Reynolds and Pogue. I'll be here after they are gone."

"And after I'm gone?"

"Maybe that, too." Pat suddenly turned again and rested his big hands on the bar. "You fool around with Pogue all you want. With Reynolds, too. But you lay off Levitt an' his crowd, you hear? They ain't human. They'll kill you. They'll eat you like a cat does a mouse, when they get ready."

"Maybe." Ross struck a match with his left hand. "Who are his crowd?"

Pat looked disgusted. "You've been to the VV. He runs that spread. Don't you be too friendly with that girl, either. She's poison."

Haney let that one ride. Maybe she was poison. Maybe feeling the way he did about her was the thing that would break him. He was a strong man. He had not lived that long under the conditions he knew without knowing his own strength and knowing how it compared with the strength of others. He knew that, when he was sure, he would push his luck to any degree, but as yet he was not pushing it, as yet no one in the valley knew his real intentions.

Pogue believed he had come looking for Chubb. Reynolds and Berdue, despite their hatred for him, believed he was after Pogue. Each was prepared to keep hands off in hopes he would injure the other. Yet the roundup was going to blow the lid off, for the roundup was going to show that he had cattle on the range, and had pitched his hat into the ring. Then he would be in the middle of the fight with every man's hand against him.

Pat's warning was right. Pogue and Reynolds were dangerous, but nothing compared to Levitt's crowd. Lifting his glass, Ross studied his reflection in the mirror, the reflection of a tall, wide-shouldered young man with blunt, bronzed features and a smile that came easily to eyes that were half-cynical, half-amused. He was a tall young man with a flat-brimmed, flat-crowned black hat and a gray, shield-chested shirt and a black knotted kerchief, black crossed belts supporting the worn holsters and walnut-stocked guns. He was a fool, he decided, to think as he did about Sherry. What could he offer such a girl? On the other hand, what could Star Levitt offer her?

Regardless, he was here to stay. When he had raced the Appaloosa into the street of Soledad, he had come to remain. If he had to back it with gunfire, he would do just that. Carefully he considered the state of his plans. There was no fault to find there. In fact, he had progressed beyond where he had expected in that he had a friend, an ally, a man who would stay with him to the last ditch. He had Rolly Burt.

Camping on the mesa, the wounded man was rapidly knitting. They had talked much, and Burt had told him what to expect of the roundup. He knew the characters and personalities of the people of the Ruby Hills, and he knew something more of Pogue and Reynolds. Over nights beside the campfire they had yarned and argued and talked. Both of them had ridden for Charles Goodnight, both for John Chisum. They knew the same saloons in Tascosa and El Paso. Both had been over the trail to Dodge and to Cheyenne. Both had been in Uvalde and Laredo, and they talked the nights away of cattle and horses, of rustling and gunfighters until they knew each other, and knew they spoke the same language. Rolly had talked much of Mabry. He was a good man. While Mabry liked both Bob and Sherry Vernon, he had confided to Burt that he must leave the VV or be killed.

"Why were the Box N boys gunnin' for you, Rolly?" he had asked.

A frown had gathered between Rolly Burt's eyes. He had looked up at Ross over the fire. His blue eyes were puzzled and disturbed. "You know, I can't figure that. It was a set deal. I saw that right away. They'd been sent to murder me."

"How'd you happen to be in town?"

"Berdue sent me in for a message."

"I see." Ross had told him then about the meeting below the mesa, and everything but Sherry's part in it. "There's a tie-up there somewhere. I think Berdue sent you on purpose, an' he had those Box N boys primed to kill you."

"But why?"

"Something you know, probably. The way I have it figured is that Syd Berdue is in some kind of a double-cross that he doesn't want Chalk to know about. Maybe he figured he'd tipped his hand somehow, and you knew too much. Voyle is in the deal with him, and I figured from the way he acted the other night in front of Pogue that he's double-crossing Walt. And I think Star Levitt is the man behind the whole thing."

"You mean a deal between Berdue and Levitt? But they are supposed to be on the outs."

"Sure, and what better cover-up? You keep an eye on the springs. They may meet again."

"Say!" Burt had glanced up. "Something I've been meaning to ask you. Several times I've heard a funny kind of rumbling, sounds like it comes out of the rock under me. You heard it?"

"Uhn-huh. Don't reckon it amounts to much, but someday we'll do some prowling. Kind of gives an *hombre* the shivers."

Standing now at the Bit and Bridle bar, Ross Haney went over that conversation. Yes, he was ahead of his plans in having such an ally as Rolly Burt.

He leaned his forearms on the hardwood and turned his head to glance out into the street. The rose of the setting sun had tinted the dusty, unpainted boards of the old building opposite with a dull glow, and beyond it, in the space between the buildings, a deep shadow had already gathered. At the rail, Río stamped his feet against a vagrant fly and blew contentedly.

It was a quiet evening. Suddenly he felt a vague nostalgia, a longing for a home he had never known, the deep, inner desire for peace, his children about him, the quiet evening rest on a wide porch after a hard day on the range, and the sound of a voice inside, a voice singing. Yet, when he straightened and filled his glass again, the guns felt heavy against his legs. Someday, with luck, things would be different.

Then the half doors pushed open, and Star Levitt stood there, tall and handsome against the facing light. He looked for an instant at Ross, and then came on into the room. He wore the same splendid white hat, a white buckskin vest, and perfectly creased gray trousers tucked into polished boots. As always, the worn guns struck the only incongruous note. His voice was easy, confident.

"Buy you a drink?"

"Thanks, I've got one." In the mirror Ross's eyes caught the difference between them, his battered shabbiness against the cool magnificence of Levitt.

Levitt's smile was pleasant, his voice ordinary and casual. "Planning to leave soon?"

"No." Haney's voice was flat. "I'm never going to leave."

"That's what the country needs, they tell me. Permanent settlers, somebody to build on. It's a nice thought, if you can stick it."

"That's right. How about you, Levitt? Do you think you'll be able to stick it when Reynolds and Pogue get to checking brands?" He heard a glass rattle in Pat's suddenly nervous fingers. He knew he had taken the play away from Levitt with that remark, and he followed it up. "I've been over the range lately, and there's a lot of steers out there with VVs made over into Three Diamonds, an' Box Ns to Triple Box As, an' I understand that brand happens to be yours, too."

Levitt had straightened and was looking at him, all the smile gone from his face. "You understand too much, Haney. You're getting into water that's too deep for you, or for any drifting cowhand."

"Am I? Let me judge. I've waded through some bad water a few times, an', where I couldn't wade, I could swim."

Star Levitt's eyes had widened and the bones seemed to stretch the skin of his face taut and hard. He was not a man used to being talked back to, and he wasn't used to being thwarted. He was shrewd, a planner, but in that instant Ross learned something else of him. He had a temper, and, when pushed, he got angry. Such a man was apt to be hasty. *All right,* Ross told himself, *let's see.*

"Another thing. You spoke the other day about a staked claim. I'm curious to see how deep your stakes are driven, so I'm going to find out for myself, Levitt. I don't think that claim is very secure. I think a little bit of bad weather an' all your stakes would shake loose. You're a big boy, Levitt, but you're not cutting the wide swath you think you are. Now you know where I stand, so don't try running any bluff on me. I won't take a pushing around."

"Stand aside, Star, an' let me have him!" The voice rang in an almost empty room, and Haney's hair prickled along his scalp as he saw Emmett Chubb standing just inside the door. "I want him, anyway, Star!"

Ross Haney stood, his feet wide apart, facing them and he knew he was in the tightest spot of his life. Two of the deadliest gunmen in the country were facing him, and he was alone. Cold and still he waited, and the air was so tense he could hear the hoarse breathing of the bartender beside him and across the bar.

So still was the air in the room that Bill Mabry's voice, low as it was, could be heard by all.

"If they want it, Haney, I'll take Star for you. He's right here under my gun."

Levitt's eyes did not waver. Haney saw the quick calculation in the big man's eyes, then saw decision. Levitt was sharp, and this situation offered nothing for anybody. It was two and two, and Mabry's position at the window from which he spoke commanded the situation perfectly, as he was just slightly behind both Levitt and Chubb.

It was Pat who broke the stalemate. "Nobody does any shootin' here unless it's me," he said flatly. "Mabry, you stand where you are. Chubb, you take your hand away from that gun an' get out of that door, face first. Star, you foller him. I ain't aimin' to put clean sawdust on this here floor again today. Now git!"

He enforced his command with the twin barrels of a shotgun over the edge of the bar, and nobody had any argument with a shotgun at close quarters. A six-gun warrants a gamble, but there is no gamble with a sawed-off scatter-gun.

Chubb turned on his heel and strode from the room, and Star smiled suddenly, but his eyes were cold as they turned to Haney. "You talk a good fight," he said. "We'll have to see what you're holding."

"All right," Ross replied shortly. "I'll help you check brands at the roundup!"

Levitt walked out, and then Bill Mabry put a foot

through the open window, and stepped into the bar. He grinned. "That job open?"

Haney laughed. "Friend, you've been working for me for the last three minutes," he declared warmly.

"You two finish your drinks and pull out," Pat said dryly. "Powder smoke gives me a headache."

Chapter Eleven

Gathered over the fire in the hollow atop the mesa, crouched three men, not daring to use the partly constructed house as the glow of the fire might attract attention. Here, in a more sheltered position far back from the rim, they could talk in quiet and without fear of the fire attracting undue attention.

Burt, whose leg was much better, was cooking. "It ain't all clear, Ross, but I think you've got the right idea. It looks like Levitt is engineerin' some kind of a steal if Voyle, Dahl, an' Berdue are in it with him. I do know this. There's been a passel of hardcases comin' into the valley here lately. They ain't tied in with the Box N or the RR by any means."

"Sure, look at Streeter an' Hanson," Mabry said. "They are with Pogue, but how far can he count on 'em? I think Streeter an' Hanson will stay out of things if Levitt says to. I think he's cut the ground from under the feet of both men."

"Those brands I've looked at aren't intended to fool anybody, it seems to me," Haney commented. "I think Levitt plans to start trouble. It's my opinion that he'll blow the lid off things just when the rest of them are standin' by for the roundup. How many reliable hands has Vernon got?"

"Three or four," Mabry replied. "Dahl and his partner ran several off. A man sure don't feel comfortable workin' around a ranch with two *hombres* on the prod like that."

"What goes on around there?" Haney asked Mabry. "You've lived on that spread, an' should know."

Mabry shrugged. "I sure don't know," he said honestly. "Seems to be a lot of movin' around at night on that spread, but Dahl or his partner are usually by the door, an' they go out to see what it's all about. Several times at night riders have showed up there, leavin' hard-ridden horses behind when they take off. No familiar brands but one. That I think I've seen down Mexico way."

Ross took the plate he was handed and dished up some fríjoles and then accepted the coffee Burt poured for him. There seemed to be but one answer. He would have to do some night riding and look around a little. After all, there couldn't be many possibilities.

"Well," Burt suggested at last, "the roundup starts tomorrow. Before it has gone very far, we'll know a lot of things."

From the rim of the mesa they watched all the following morning. Reynolds's hands were rounding up cattle, driving them out of the timber and down into the flat. Some of the Box N riders were part of the group.

The weather was hot and dry, and dust arose in clouds. The cattle moved from the shade and ample water of the springs with reluctance. As always, it gave Ross a thrill to watch the cattle gathered and to see a big herd moving. He kept back and out of sight but took turns with Mabry at watching the work.

Regardless of their sympathies, there were good cattlemen on both sides. The riders got the cattle out of the brakes and started them downvalley to the accompaniment of many yells, much shouting back and forth, and the usual good-natured persiflage and joking that is part of any roundup crew. As far as Ross's glass was able to see, the same thing was happening everywhere. There would be several thousand head of stock to work in this roundup, and it would move on down the range for many miles before completed.

Mabry slid up alongside of him at noon on the second day. "You want me to rep for you, or will you tackle it your own self?"

Haney thought a minute. "We'll both go down, but we'll go loaded for bear. I think hell is going to break loose down there before many days."

"If they start to fight, what do we do?" Mabry asked keenly,

"Pull out. We don't have a battle with any of them. Not yet, we don't, but almost any of them might take a shot at us. When they see what's happened, that I've got cattle on this range, they aren't going to be too happy about it."

"Have you seen Scott?"

"Only for a minute or two. He's advisin' me to get more hands, but I don't want anybody killed, neither of you nor myself, either. If there's only three of us, we'll play our cards the way we should, close to our belt. If there were more, we might take chances and get somebody killed. If they start a battle, pull out."

"Don't you rate that Levitt too low, Haney." Mabry shook his head seriously. "He's cold-blooded, and he'll do whatever he's a mind to, to get his way on this range. He hasn't any use for either Pogue or Reynolds, but he's a sight worse than either of them."

It was good advice, and the following day, when the two drifted down off the mesa toward the roundup, Ross Haney was thinking about it.

"Remember one thing," he advised Mabry. "We may not be together all the time. Don't let yourself get sucked in. Hold to the outer edge all the time, and keep an eye on the hands we've talked about who we believe to be tied in with Levitt. I wouldn't be surprised at anything. If they start scattering out, and seem to be taking up any definite positions, ease out of there quick."

Walt Pogue looked unhappy when he saw the two riding up. Then he brightened noticeably. "You two hunting work? I need some men."

"No." Haney noted that Chalk Reynolds was riding over. "I've come to rep for my brand."

Pogue's head came down and his eyes squinted. He leaned toward them, and his somewhat thick lips parted. "Did you say . . . *your* brand?"

"That's right . . . the Gallows Frame."

The big rancher's face went white, then darkened with a surge of blood. He reined his horse around violently. "Who said you could run cattle on this range?"

Ross Haney shrugged. Chalk Reynolds looked as astonished and angry as Pogue. "Does anybody have to say so? Strikes me this here is government land, and my stock has as much right to run on it as yours, an' maybe more right."

"You'll find there's a difference of opinion on that!" Chalk Reynolds put in violently. "This range is overcrowded now."

"Tell that to Star Levitt. He's on it with two brands."

This was obviously no news to either of them, but neither had anything to say for a minute, and then Reynolds said coldly: "Well, he'll be told! From what I hear, somebody's doin' some mighty smooth work with a cinch ring!"

Ross hooked his leg around the saddle horn and began to dig for the makings. "Reynolds, if you an' Pogue will take a look at those altered brands, you'll see that whoever altered them doesn't give a hoot whether you know it or not. He's throwin' it right in your face, an'askin' what you intend to do."

"I'll do plenty!" Chalk bellowed. "There's goin' to be a new set-up on this range after this roundup is over!"

"You throwin' that at me?" Pogue demanded. Fury was building in the man, and he was staring at Reynolds with an ugly light in his eye.

"Why don't you two either go to it or cut it out?" Haney drawled. "Or are you both afraid of Levitt? He's the *hombre* who's cuttin' in on you. He doesn't even bother to bring his own cows, he brands yours."

Ross chuckled, and Reynolds's face went white. He turned and said flatly, the rage trembling behind his even tones: "We might get together, Walt an' I, long enough to get shut of you!"

"Take first things first," Ross said. "An' you'd better learn this right now, Chalk. An' you, too, Pogue. I came here to stay. If you fellows stay here, it will be with me alongside of you. If you go, I'll still be here. I didn't come to this valley by chance. I came here on purpose, and with a definite idea in mind. Any bet you make, I'll double and raise. So any time you want to get into the game with me, just start the ball rolling, anyway you like."

He struck a match and lighted his smoke, then dropped his leg back and kicked his foot into the stirrup. Coolly, and without a backward glance, he rode away.

Bill Mabry sat quietly for a minute or two, watching him ride.

Pogue glared at him. "What's in this, Bill? You've always been a good man."

"You listen to him," Mabry advised dryly. "He's *mucho malo hombre*, if you get what I mean. But only when he's crossed. He's got no reason to like either of you, but he's got other things on his mind now. But in case either of you wonder where I stand. Me an' my six-gun, we stand right alongside of Ross Haney. And that's where you'll find Rolly Burt, too!"

"Burt?" Pogue's face flamed. "Where is that murderin' son-of-a-bitch?"

Bill Mabry turned, his hand on the cantle of the saddle: "Listen, why don't you find out why two of your men were gunning for him, Pogue? I'll bet a paint pony you don't know. An' why don't you, Chalk Reynolds, find out why none of your boys was in town that night to side Burt? Why did your nephew send him into town for a message?"

Mabry turned and cantered his horse over to Ross. "I gave 'em some more," he said briefly, and explained.

Haney chuckled. "Their ears will be buzzing for a week if they live that long. Some nice stock here, Bill, at that."

"How many head have you got out here?"

"Not many. Couple of dozen head is all. Just something to make them unhappy."

"Suppose they start to get sore? Reynolds an' Pogue both can be mighty mean."

"We'll get meaner. I've got them cold-decked, Bill. Someday I'll tell you about it. I've got them all cold-decked. The only way they can beat me in the long run is with hot lead."

"Maybe. But that Star Levitt is poison."

"You think Pogue and Reynolds will get through the roundup without a fight?"

"No. There's too much hard feelin' amongst the boys. Somebody will blow his top and then the whole thing will bust up in a shootin' match."

Ross Haney looked across the valley, watching the familiar scene with a little of the old lift within him. This was the roundup, the hardest work in a cowhand's life, and in many ways the highest point. They cussed the roundup, and loved it. It was hot, dusty, full of danger from kicking hoofs and menacing horns, but filled with good fellowship and comradely fun.

The waving sea of horns tossed and rolled and fell as the cattle milled or the herd, starting to line out for somewhere, anywhere, was turned back on itself by some cowhand quick to stop the movement. At such times the horns would send a long ripple of movement across the herd.

Wild-eyed steers lunged for a getaway, but were quickly harried back into the herd. At the branding pens men were gathered, the sharp line of demarcation between the RR and Box N a little broken here by the business of the day. Elsewhere, the men from the two big outfits drew off by themselves, worked together, and avoided contact with the rival ranch hands.

Star Levitt, astride a magnificent white horse, was everywhere to be seen. For a time, he was at the branding pens, and then he was circling the herd. Finally, sighting Ross Haney and Mabry, he walked his horse toward them. Ross saw Mabry stiffen and his face tighten and grow cold. Certainly there was no love lost here.

"How are you, Haney?" Levitt was easy, casual. He seemed to have forgotten completely the events of the day in the Bit and Bridle. He was clean-shaven as always, and as always he was immaculate. The dust of the roundup seemed scarcely to have touched him.

Mabry, glancing at the two, was struck for the first time at something strikingly similar in the two men, only there was a subtle difference that drew the cowhand inexorably to Ross Haney. Both were big men, Levitt the taller and heavier, and probably somewhat softer. Ross was lean and hard, his rugged build seeming so lean as to belie his actual weight, which was some 200 pounds. Yet in the faces of both men there was the look of command. Haney's manner was easy, even careless, yet there was something solid about him, something rock-like that was lacking in the brittle sharpness of Star Levitt.

These two were shaped by nature to be enemies, two strong men with their faces turned in the same direction, yet backed by wholly varied thinking. The one ruthless and relentless, willing to take any advantage, willing to stop at nothing. The other, hard, toughened by range wars and fighting, with the rough-handed fair play of the Western plains, yet equally relentless. It could be something, Mabry thought, if they ever came together in physical combat.

Ross began building a smoke. "Looks like a good herd. You got many cows here?"

"Quite a few." Levitt glanced at him sharply. "I hear you have some, too. That you're running the Gallows Frame brand."

"That's right." Ross lighted his smoke and eased his seat on the Appaloosa. "It's a good brand."

"Seems so. Strange that I hadn't heard of any cattle coming into the country lately. Did you pick yours up on the range?"

At many times in many places such a remark would have meant shooting. After Haney's equally insulting remarks in the Bit and Bridle, they were not important. These two knew their time was coming, and neither was in a rush. Levitt was completely, superbly confident. Ross was hard and determined, his hackles raised by this man, his manner always verging on outright aggressiveness.

"No, I didn't need to. Your pattern suits you, mine suits me." He inhaled deeply and let the smoke trickle out through his nostrils. "My cattle were already here."

The remark drew the response he wanted. It was a quick, nervous, and irritable scowl from Levitt. "That's impossible!" he said. "Only three brands ran on this range until I moved in!"

Haney smiled, knowing his enigmatic smile and manner would infuriate Levitt. "Star," he drawled, "you're an *hombre* that figures he's right smart, an' you might be if you didn't figure the other fellow was so all-fired dumb. A man like you ain't got a chance to win for long in any game for that reason. You take everybody for bein' loco or dumb as a month-old calf. You ride into everything full of confidence an' sneers. You're like most crooks. You think everything will turn out right for you. Why, you're so wrong it don't need any argument. You came into this country big an' strong. You were goin' to be the boss. You saw Reynolds an' Pogue, an' you figured them for easy marks. You maybe had something on the Vernons. I haven't figured that out yet, but like so many crooks you overlooked the obvious.

"Let me tell you something, my cut-throat friend, an' get it straight. You lost this fight before you started. You might win with bullets, that's still anybody's guess, but you'll lose. You're smart in a lot of ways, an', if you were really smart you'd turn that horse of yours and start out of this country an' never stop until you're five hundred miles east of Tascosa."

Levitt smiled, but the smile was forced. For the first time the big man was uneasy, yet it was only for a moment. "I may not be as smart as I think, Haney, but no four-bit cowhand is going to outsmart me."

Ross turned slightly. "Bill, let's drift down toward the pens. I want to see what Reynolds an' Pogue think of those altered brands."

Chapter Twelve

Nonchalantly Haney turned his back on Levitt and started away. Mabry rode beside him, occasionally stealing a glance his way. "Boss, you're sure turnin' the knife in that *hombre*. What you aimin' to do, force his hand?"

"Somethin' like that. It does me good just to goad him. But you keep your eyes open, because he's got something cookin' now. I only wish"—his brow creased with worry—"I knew what he had on the Vernons. You don't suppose she really cares for that *hombre*, do you?"

Mabry shrugged. "I can guess what a fool cow will do, an' I can outguess a bronc', but keep me away from women. I never could read the sign right to foller their trail. Just when you think you can read the brand, they turn the other way an' it looks altogether different."

Despite the growing sense of danger, the roundup was moving very well, yet the tenseness of the riders for all the brands was becoming increasingly evident. Several times Ross saw Sherry, but she avoided him. Bob Vernon was there, working like any of his men, and showing himself to be a fair hand, and a very willing one. Yet, as his eyes roved the herd and searched the faces of the riders, Ross could see that under the heat, the irritating, confusing dust, and the hard labor tempers were growing short.

On the third day, when the roundup had moved to the vicinity of Soledad, the break came. Ross had been trying to find a chance to talk to Sherry, and suddenly he saw it. The girl had been talking with Levitt. She had started away from him, riding toward the cottonwoods that marked the VV ranch house.

Ross started after her, and noticed Kerb Dahl, his hard, lupine face set grimly, staring after him. Dahl had drawn aside from the crowd and was building a smoke. Mabry, who had been working hard all morning, was still in the center of things, but Voyle was saddling a fresh horse.

Haney overtook Sherry and she looked up at him. He noticed for the first time how thin she had grown and how white her face was.

"Sherry?" Surprisingly his voice was unsteady. "Wait a minute."

She drew up, waiting for him, but he thought she waited without any desire for conversation. She said nothing as he rode alongside. "Leaving so soon?"

She nodded. "Star said the men were getting pretty rough in their talk, and they'd be more comfortable if I went in."

"I've been hoping I'd have a chance to talk to

you. You've been avoiding me." His eyes were accusing, but bantering.

She looked at him directly then. "Yes, Ross, I have. We must not see each other again. I'm going to marry Star, and seeing you won't do."

"You don't love him." The statement was flat and level, but she avoided his glance, and made no response. Then suddenly she said: "Ross, I've got to go. Star insisted I leave right away."

Haney's eyes hardened. "Do you take orders from him? What is this, anyway? Are you a slave? Haven't you a chance to make up your own mind?" Her face reddened and she was about to make a quick, and probably angry retort, when her remark hit him. He seized her wrist. "Sherry, you say Star insisted? That you leave *now?*"

"Yes." She was astonished and puzzled by his expression. "He said. . . ."

The remark trailed off, for Ross Haney had turned sharply in his saddle. Kerb Dahl had finished his cigarette. Voyle was fumbling with his saddle girth, and for the first time Haney noticed that he carried a rifle in his saddle scabbard, a rifle within inches of his hands. Ross's eyes strayed for the white horse, and found it on the far side.

He turned quickly. "Sherry, he's right. Get back to the ranch as fast as you can, and don't leave it!"

He wheeled his horse and started back toward the branding pens at a rapid canter, hoping he would be in time. A small herd of cattle was drifting down toward the pens, and behind it were Streeter and Repp Hanson.

As he drew up on the edge of the branding, Mabry was just straightening up from slapping a brand on a steer. "Bill!" Haney had to call three times before Mabry heard him, and then the red-headed cowhand turned and walked toward him. "Look out, Bill! It's coming."

His remark might have been a signal, for Emmett Chubb, sitting his horse near the corral on the outside of the pole fence, spoke up and pointed his remark at Riggs, a Box N rider. "You all feet, or just nat'rally dumb?"

Riggs looked up sharply. "What's the matter with you, Chubb? I haven't seen you down here doin' any work!"

Riggs was a slim, hard-faced youngster and a top hand. His anger was justifiable and he was not thinking or caring who or what Chubb was. Riggs had worked while the gunman lounged in his saddle, carrying his perpetual sneer.

"Shucks," Chubb said, "you Box N hands done enough work afore the roundup, slappin' brands on everythin' in sight! Bunch of tinhorn cow thieves!"

"You're a liar!" Riggs snapped, and Chubb's hand flashed for his gun. At that, Riggs almost made it. His gun was coming up when Chubb's first shot smashed him in the middle. He staggered back, gasping fiercely, struggling to get his gun up.

Instantly the branding pens were bursting with gunfire. Mabry swung into the saddle and whipped his horse around the corner of the stock pens, and he and Ross Haney headed for the timber. "It's their fight," Mabry said bitterly. "Let them have it."

"Look!" Haney was pointing.

Mabry glanced over his shoulder as the firing burst out, and his face went hard and cold.

Streeter and Hanson from their saddles had opened up on Reynolds and Pogue. Voyle was firing over the saddle of his horse, and cattle were scattering in every direction. Dust arose in a thick cloud. From it came the scream of a man in agony, then another burst of firing.

Mabry gasped out an oath. The freckles were standing out against the dead white of his face. "Pogue's own men turned on him!"

"Yeah." Ross Haney hurled his cigarette into the dust. "We'd better light a shuck. I think they intended to get us, too!"

The crash of guns stopped suddenly, but the scene was obscured by dust from the crazed cattle and excited horses. Ross saw a riderless horse, stirrups flapping, come from the dust cloud, head high and reins trailing. Behind them there was a single shot, then another.

Finally, with miles behind them, Mabry looked over at Ross. "I feel like a coyote ridin' away from a fight, like that, but it sure wasn't none of ours."

Haney nodded grimly. "I saw it comin' but never guessed it would break out just like that. It couldn't be stopped without killin' Levitt."

"You think he engineered it?"

"Sure." Haney explained how Levitt had started Sherry home, and how his riders had moved out of the workingmen's group to good firing positions. "Chubb had his orders. He deliberately started that fight when he got the signal."

"I'll get him if it's the last thing I do!" Mabry

said bitterly. "That Riggs was a good hand. We hunted strays together."

"There was nothing we could have done but stay there an' die. We've got other things to do, Bill. We've got to see that Levitt's plans go haywire an' that he gets his desserts. We've got to get the Vernons out from under. Star will have this country sewed up now, with no one able to buck him but us. He'll rave when he finds we got away."

"As far as Reynolds an' Pogue," Mabry said, "I can't feel no sorrow. They were a couple of murderin' wolves, but they had some good men ridin' for 'em." Mabry scowled. "Wonder what Levitt will do now? He's got the range sewed up with them two out of the way an' the Vernons knucklin' under to him."

Ross frowned. He had thought that over and believed he knew the answer. "That we'll have to wait an' see," he said. "I'm right curious myself. He'll hunt us, an' we'll have to lay low. He'll blame the whole thing on the feud between the two big outfits an' claim he was just an innocent bystander."

"What about the riders?" Mabry protested. "Some of them will tell the truth!"

"Bill," Haney said, "I'd lay a good bet none of them know. We knew pretty well what was comin', an' moreover we got off to one side with a clear view. Down there among the stampedin' cows, the dust, an' shootin', I'll bet the ones who are alive won't know. Moreover, I'll bet most of them drift out of the country. If they don't drift, Levitt will probably see that they do. From his standpoint it's foolproof. Remember, too, that Levitt's gunmen were men from both outfits."

"If he kills like that," Mabry asked, "what chance have three men got?"

"The best chance, Bill. We're still honest men even if the only law is gun law. We'll wait an' see what Levitt does, but I imagine the first thing he'll do will be to clean up the loose ends. He may even call in the law from outside so he'll be in the clear with a clean bill of health."

Rolly Burt was waiting for them when they rode in. "What happened?" he demanded. "Did the lid blow off? I heard shootin'."

Briefly Haney explained. "The fight would have come, I expect, even if Levitt hadn't planned it."

"How many were killed?"

"No tellin'. I doubt if so many. Enough to warrant Levitt playin' the big, honest man who wants to keep the peace. Down there in the dust, I doubt if anybody scored many good shots. Too much confusion and too many running cattle. Riggs is probably dead."

"Murderin' coyotes!" Burt limped to the fire. "Set and eat. I've got the grub ready."

He dished up the food, then straightened, fork in hand. "Ross, what happened to Chalk?"

Haney did not look up. "He's sure to be dead. So's Pogue. Even Syd Berdue was shootin' at them. Killed his own uncle, or lent a hand."

"Chalk was no good, but no man deserves that." Burt looked up suddenly. "Boss, while you two were gone, I done some stumpin' around to loosen the muscles in this here game leg, an' guess what I found?"

"What?" Haney dished up a forkful of beans, then looked over it at Rolly, struck by something in his tone.

"That rumblin' in the rock . . . I found what causes it!" he said. "An' man, when you see it, your hair'll stand on end, I'm tellin' you!"

Chapter Thirteen

Yawning, Ross Haney opened his eyes to look through the aspen leaves at a cloudless sky. The vast expanse of blue stretched above them as yet unfired by the blazing heat of the summer sun. He rolled out of his soogan and dressed, trying to keep his feet out of the dew covering the grass.

Bill Mabry stuck a head bristling with red hair, all standing on end, out of his blankets and stared unhappily at Haney.

"Rolly," he complained, "what can a man do when his boss gets up early? It ain't neither fittin' nor right, I say."

"Pull your head back in then, you sorrel-topped bronc'!" Haney growled. "I'm goin' to have a look at the valley, an' then Rolly can roll out an' scare up some chuck."

"How about this all-fired rumblin'?" Mabry sat up. "I heard it again last night. Gives a man the creeps."

Burt sat up and looked around for his boots. He

rubbed his unshaven jowls as he did every morning and muttered: "Dang it, I need a shave!"

"Never seen you when you didn't." Mabry thrust his thumb through a hole in his sock and swore, then pulled it on. "You need a haircut, too, you durned Siwash. Ugly, that's what you are! What a thing to see when you first wake up! Lucky you never hitched up with no girl. She sure would have had you curried and combed to a fare-thee-well!"

Ross left them arguing and, picking up his glass, walked to the nest of boulders he used for a lookout. Settling down on his stomach in the sand, he pointed the glass down the valley.

At first, all seemed serene and beautiful. The morning sunlight sparkled on the pool below, and the sound of the running water came to his ears. Somewhere, far off, a cow bawled. He swept the edge of the trees close at hand, studied the terrain below, and then bit by bit he eased his line of quest up until he was looking well downrange toward the Soledad trail.

The sun felt good on his back, and he squirmed to shift his position a little, leveled the glass, then froze.

A group of horsemen was coming up the trail toward Thousand Springs, riding slowly. Star Levitt, he made out, was not among them. As they drew nearer, he picked out first one, and then another. They were led by Syd Berdue, and Kerb Dahl and Voyle were with him. Also, Emmett Chubb and half a dozen other riders. As they drew rein below him and let their horses drink, a few words drifted up to him.

This time they were making no secret of their

conversation, and in the bright morning air their words were, for the most part, plain enough.

"Beats all where he got to!" Dahl replied. "I never did see Star so wrought up about anythin' as when he found they'd got away. He must have turned over everything in the flat, a-huntin' 'em. Refused to believe they'd got away. Golly was he mad!"

"He's a bad man to cross," Streeter commented. "I never seen him mad before. He goes crazy."

Chubb hung at one edge of the group, taking no part in their talking. His eyes strayed toward Berdue from time to time. Finally he swung down and walked to one of the springs for a drink, and, when he came back, wiping his mouth, his eyes shifted from one to the other. "Some things about this I don't like," he said.

There was no reply. Watching, Ross had the feeling that Chubb expressed the view of more than one of them. Syd idly flicked his quirt at a mesquite.

"Well, you can't say he ain't thorough," he said grimly.

Chubb looked around. "Yeah," he agreed sarcastically. "But how thorough? Where does his bein' thorough stop? You ever start to figure like that? He had me primed to start the play by gunnin' Riggs, as he had Riggs pegged as a hot head who would go for a gun if pushed. Well, I hadn't no use for Riggs my ownself, but he never told me what was to come after. It was pure luck I didn't get killed."

"Where did you reckon Haney went?" Dahl demanded, changing the subject.

"Where did Rolly Burt go?" Voyle asked. "You ask me, that Ross Haney is nobody's fool. He an' Mabry sure got shut of those brandin' pens in a hurry. They lit out like who flunk the chunk. Maybe left the country."

"He shore didn't," Chubb said bitterly. "He wants my scalp. He'll not leave if I read his tracks right."

"He called the boss a couple of times," Voyle said. "Pogue, too. Don't seem to take no water for anybody."

Syd Berdue's eyes shifted from face to face, waiting for somebody to mention his own fuss with Haney, but they avoided his eyes. "I'd say the thing to do would be to stop chasin' over the country an' keep an eye on that Kinney feller. He was right friendly with Haney, they tell me."

"Or Sherry Vernon," Dahl sneered. "I think the boss is buckin' a stacked deck with her."

Watching from the mesa, and listening to the faint sound of their voices, Ross could see Kerb Dahl's eyes shifting from man to man. He shook his own head, disgusted. *They talk too much,* he told himself. *That Dahl will tell Levitt every word or I miss my guess. He wasn't planted on the VV for nothing.*

Long after the group rode away, he lay there restlessly, hoping for some sight of Sherry, but there was none. More than he cared to admit, he was worried about her. Star Levitt had been revealed as a much more ruthless man, and a more cruel man than he had believed. Perhaps of them all, Emmett Chubb was the nearest to correct in his estimation of Levitt's character.

There was small chance he would ever allow any

group below to escape the valley to talk and repeat what they knew over too many glasses of whiskey. He was thorough, and he would be thorough enough, and hard enough, to carry out what he had started.

Yet there was little Haney could do until Levitt's next move was revealed. Reynolds and Pogue were gone and the Ruby Hills country lay in the big man's palm. Haney longed for a talk with Scott, for the old storekeeper was a shrewd judge of men, and he listened much and heard everything.

Returning to the fire, he joined Burt and Mabry in eating a quick breakfast. "Now," he said as he finished his last cup of coffee, "we'll see what you've got to show us. Then Mabry an' me will go down into the lava an' push out some more cows. We've got to keep Levitt sweatin'."

Burt, whose leg was rapidly returning to normal, led them through the aspens to the open mesa, and then along its top toward the jumbled maze of boulders that blocked off any approach from the northwest except by the narrow trail Haney used in coming and going.

The way Burt took followed a dim pathway into the boulders and ended at a great leaning slab of granite under which there was a dark, chill-looking opening.

"Come on," he said. "We're going down here!" He had brought with him several bits of candle, and now he passed one to each of them. They stooped, and crept into the hole. The air felt damp inside, and there was a vast, cavernous feeling as of a dark, empty space. Holding their candles high, they saw they were on a steep floor that led away ahead of them, going down and down into an abysmal darkness from which came the faint sound of falling water.

Burt hobbled along ahead of them, and they had descended seventy or eighty feet below the level of the mesa above, when he paused on the rim of a black hole. Leaning forward, Ross Haney saw a bottomless blackness from which there came at intervals a strange sighing, and then a low rumble.

"We got maybe ten minutes, the way I figure it," Burt said. "And then to be on the safe side, we've got to get out." He knelt and touched the rock at the edge of the hole. "Look how smooth. Water done that, water falling on it for years and years. I tried to time it yesterday, an' it seems to come about every three hours. Pressure must build away down inside the mountain somehow, an' then she blows a cork an' water comes a spoutin' an' a spumin' out of this hole. She shoots cl'ar up, nigh to the roof, and she keeps a spoutin' for maybe three, four minutes. Then it dies away, an' that's the end."

"Well, I'm dog-goned!" Mabry exclaimed. "I've heard about this place. Injuns used to call it the Talkin' Mountain. Heard the Navajos speak of it afore I ever came over here."

"Stones come up on that water, too, an' water fills this whole room, just boilin' an' roarin', but that ain't all. Look up there!" He stepped back and pointed, and, moving away from the rim, they looked up.

High above them, in the vaulted top of the cave

were several ragged holes. "Back in the trees, too! A man could walk right into them if he wasn't careful, an' he'd go right on through into that, or else break a leg an' lie on the rim until the water came."

"Ugly-lookin'," Ross said. "Let's get out of here."

They turned and started out, and then from behind them came a dull, mounting rumble!

"Run!" Burt's face was suddenly panic-stricken. "Here it comes!"

He lunged forward and, scrambling, fell full length on the steep trail. Haney stooped and grabbed the man, but he was a big man and powerful, and unless Bill Mabry had not grabbed the other arm he never would have gotten him up the steep hole in time.

They scrambled out into the sunlight, their faces pale, and below and behind them they heard the pound and rumble of boulders and the roar of water tumbling in the vast and empty cavern.

"That," Mabry said dryly, "is a good place to keep out of!"

When they returned to the camp, Burt started for his horse. "I'll saddle up," he said, "an' help you *hombres*. I've been loafin' long enough."

"You stay here." Ross turned around and grinned at him. "You keep an eye on the springs, as I've a hunch we'll have more visitors. This is a two-man job. Tomorrow, if we need help, you can go an' we'll leave Bill behind, or I'll stay."

Mabry had little to say on the ride into the lava beds, but Haney was just as pleased for his thoughts were busy with Sherry and the situation in the valley and at Soledad. He made up his mind he would take a chance and slip into town. Then he could talk to Scott or Kinney, and would be able to find out just what was taking place.

He had no idea what had happened beyond the few words he could catch from the conversation of the posse searching for him, but Scott would know all that had happened. On second thought, it would be wiser to see only Scott, for the chances were that Kinney would be watched. Already the connection with him would be formed in Star Levitt's mind.

The work in the lava beds was hot and tiring. The wild cattle fought like devils and branding them was a slow task and a hazardous one for the two men. Yet by nightfall they had branded enough of them to warrant their work. They camped at night in the cañon, and the following morning started the cattle out through the deep crevasse toward open range. Once they had them started toward Thousand Springs, they returned to the mesa where Rolly was waiting for them.

"Took a ride in last night," he volunteered, "been goin' stale layin' around. I talked to Kinney a little, but they're watchin' him."

"What's happened?" Haney's irritation at Burt's gamble was lost in his eagerness for news.

"Well, Levitt seems to be havin' everythin' his own way. He made Emmett Chubb sheriff, and says it's goin' to be necessary to be strict until they rid themselves of the lawless elements, which probably means us. I talked to Scott, an' he sure wants to see you. Sherry Vernon ain't been seen in town since the fight, an' Bob only oncet, an' then he came an' hightailed it out of there. Levitt, he sent for outside law."

"He did what?"

"Sent for some outside law. He says he aims to have this Reynolds an' Pogue feud cleared up, an' he wants you caught. Says you're a rustler, an' may have had more than a little hand in the killin' at the stock pens. He wants the blame fixed, he says. Also, the story's around"—Burt cleared his throat and avoided Haney's eyes—"that there will be a weddin' out at the VV pretty soon."

Ross stared at the fire. So that was it? Now he would marry Sherry Vernon and the VV would be his in name as well as in appearances, for once they were married he would know how to handle Bob. If Haney was to do anything, it must be done soon. It must be done now.

"Howsoever, there seems to be some talk around. Syd Berdue ain't happy with the new set-up. Kerb Dahl is foreman at the VV, an' Chubb is sheriff. Bob Streeter is foreman on the RR, an' they say Berdue fair raised mischief over that, but Levitt told him he would be taken care of."

"I reckon that's what he's scared of," Mabry said dryly. "I know what I'd do if Star Levitt said I was to be taken care of. I'd either get me a shot at Star or a fast horse out of the country."

"Well, Berdue ain't leavin'. Not willin', anyway. I reckon Star is anxious to have everything looking shipshape for the law when it comes up. They'll be glad to get shut of the trouble anyway, an', if things look pretty, they'll leave them as they be."

Ross pondered the news. Certainly Levitt's position was good. He was a smooth-talking man with a good outward appearance, and, if everything looked settled and calm, the outsiders would go away. The valley would be safely in Levitt's hands, and Ross Haney would be declared an outlaw and hunted by the forces of the law wherever he happened to appear.

It was, apparently, time to come off the mesa and enter the game once more. Suddenly he knew just exactly what he was going to do!

"Somethin' else," Burt added, "there's a lot of talk around about those steers of yours. Seems to be a lot of difference of view as to where they come from. No other brands on 'em, but full-growed steers. There's a rumor around that you've had a herd in the hills for some time."

"Bill," Ross said thoughtfully, "there's been some talk about another man on the VV spread. And when I was out there, I saw a small cabin off across the wash. You know anything about that?"

"No, I don't know anything at all. There's somethin' mighty peculiar about that cabin, an' none of us ever went near it but Star or Kerb Dahl."

Mabry leaned back against a tree and built a smoke. "Dahl, he acted mighty skittish around that cabin, his own self."

When morning came again to the Ruby Hills, Ross Haney mounted the Appaloosa and started by a winding route toward Soledad. He had no intention of getting there before dark unless it could be managed without being seen. While he was about it, he would investigate that mysterious cabin, and learn once and for all if it had anything to do with Sherry and her attitude toward Levitt.

The trail he was using was the same used on the previous trips, a trail that lay along a concealed route through the timber, mountain, and chaparral. It was the trail of which he had learned from the same source as provided the story of the cattle, the lava beds, and the mesa. This might well be the last time he would travel it for he needed no additional warning to let him know that every man's hand would be against him in Soledad.

His own position in the valley was a good one, but must be backed by gun power, and he could not match Levitt as to numbers. However, Levitt himself was bringing the law in, and the law outweighed the brute force of any outlaw or the tricks of any criminal working beyond it.

Chapter Fourteen

Circling around Soledad, he cut down through the chaparral to a position on the point of the ragged hills that overlooked the VV. Then, glass in hand, he took a comfortable position where he could watch all movement on the ranch and began a systematic survey of the entire area below.

The isolated cabin he located without trouble. He studied it for a long time, watching for any evidence of life, but found none. The cabin looked bare and lonely, and no smoke came from its small chimney, nor did anyone approach it. Obviously the cabin held something or someone of great importance to Levitt or it would not be kept so secret.

After a careful survey of the ranch buildings, he decided the door of the cabin was not actually in view of the ranch house, for that view was cut off by the stable and several large stacks of hay for feeding saddle stock through the winter months.

Kerb Dahl was loitering around the ranch yard and he was wearing two guns, but no one else was in view. Once, as dusk drew nearer, he saw Bob Vernon come to the door of the house and stare off toward town, but he turned then without coming outside, and walked back. But in that moment when he had stood in the door, Dahl had walked hastily forward and stood facing him, for all the world like a prison guard.

The evening faded and the stars came out. From away on the desert a soft wind picked up and began to blow gently. Back over the mountains lay a dark curtain of cloud, black and somber. As he glanced that way, Haney saw its bulging billows darting with sudden lightning, and once, like the whimper of far-off trumpets, he heard the distant sound of thunder.

He waited there, his ears attuned to every sound, his eyes roving over the ranch and all its approaches. In what he saw and heard now his life might depend, for in a matter of minutes he was going down there. Yet, aside from the restless roving of Kerb Dahl, there was no evidence of life about the ranch until a light came on. And when that light brightened the windows, Ross got to his feet, brushed the sand from his clothes, and stretched.

Then, leading his horse, he came off the hill, concealed from the ranch by the point of the ridge on which he had waited. He took a winding route up a sandy wash toward the ranch, stopping from time to time to listen once more, then moving on. In the shadows back of the stable, he let the horse stand, reins trailing, with a light touch on the shoulder and a whisper of warning. Nothing now but Haney's own shrill whistle would move him from the spot.

Loosening his guns in their holsters, Ross Haney took a deep breath and turned his eyes on the lonely cabin. Then he went down into the gully and started for the cabin door.

Stark and alone on the knoll it stood, a gloomy little building that seemed somehow ominous and strange. Nearby, he crouched in the darkness listening for any sound of movement that might warn him of a possible occupant. Wind whispered around the eaves and from the ranch house itself there came a rattle of dishes, the sound made plain by that cool night air. Here at the cabin all was silence. The only window was covered with a fragment of sacking, so after a long minute he moved to the door.

His heart pounded against his ribs, and his mouth felt dry. He paused, flattened against the building, and listened once more. Only the wind made a sound to be heard, a soft soughing that seemed to whisper of the impending rain. The clouds towered in the sky now, higher and closer, and the rumble of thunder was close, like a lonely lion, growling in his chest as he paced his cage.

Carefully his hand went to the knob. In the darkness the metal seemed strangely chill. His right hand moved back to his gun butt, and then, ever so carefully, he turned the knob.

It was locked.

Gently he released the knob. The pause irritated him. He had built himself to a crisis that was frustration in this most obvious of ways, and the piling up of suspense made him reckless. A glance toward the ranch assured him he was unobserved, and probably could not be seen against the blackness along the cabin wall.

This was a puzzle he must solve, and now was the time. There might never be another. Behind the locked door might lie the answer to the mystery, and he moved forward suddenly, and placed his shoulder against the flimsy panel. Light streamed from the bunkhouse windows, too. From the ranch there came only the continuing rattle of dishes, and once a loud splash as someone threw water out onto the ground. Taking the knob in his hand, he turned it, and then putting his shoulder to the door and digging his feet into the earth, he began to push.

The construction was flimsy enough. Evidently whatever was kept there was guarded by Dahl or his partner. Haney relaxed, took in a deep breath, and then putting his shoulder to the door again, he shoved hard. Something cracked sharply, and he drew back, hand on his gun, waiting and listening.

From within there came no sound. From the ranch, all was normal. He put his shoulder again to the door and heaved, but this time the damage had been done and the door came open so suddenly that he sprawled on hands and knees inside!

Cat-like, he wheeled, back to the door and gun in hand. His eyes wide for the darkness, he stared about. The light wind caught the sacking with a ghostly hand and stirred it faintly. Lightning flashed, and the room lay bare before him for an instant.

A wooden chair on its side, a worn table with an

empty basin, a cot covered with odorous blankets, and against the wall several stacks of boxes.

Puzzled, Haney crossed to them. They were not heavy. He hesitated to risk the screech of a drawn nail, but by this time he was almost beyond caring. With his fingers, he got a grip on one of the boards that made up the box, and pulled hard. It held, and then, as he strained, it came loose. If it made any sound, it was lost in the convenient rumble of thunder.

Inside the box there was more sacking, and, when that was parted, several round cans, slightly larger and not unlike a snuff can. Lifting one to his nostrils, he sniffed curiously, and from the box came a strange, pungent, half-forgotten odor.

So that's it! he thought. Then he scowled into the darkness. It did not clarify the position of Sherry, or her brother. And yet, his heart seemed to go empty within him—maybe it did!

Pocketing several of the boxes, he replaced the boards as well as he could and turned the box so as to conceal the more obvious damage. Then he slipped outside and pulled the door to behind him.

Confused by the unexpected turn of events, he returned to his horse, whispered reassuringly, and then went around the stable toward the house.

Nearby was a window, and he moved up under the trees and looked through into what was the dining room of the ranch house. Three people sat at the table. Bob and Sherry Vernon, and, at the head of the table, Star Levitt.

The window was slightly open, and he could hear their voices. Levitt was speaking: "Yes, I think that's the only solution, my dear." His tone was suave, cruel, but decisive. "We shall be married in this house on Monday. You understand?"

"You can't get away with this!" Bob burst out angrily, but the undercurrent of hopelessness in his voice was plain. "It's a devil of a thing! Sherry hates you! What sort of a mind can you have?"

"Sherry will change." Levitt smiled across the table at her. "I promise you both, she will change. Also, it will be convenient for her to be my wife. She cannot testify against me, and I scarcely believe that with her as my wife you'll care to bring any charges, Bob. Also, I'll have control of this ranch, and, as the others are in my hands, the situation is excellent."

"I've a good notion to . . . !" Bob's voice trailed off into sullenness.

"Have you?" Levitt glanced up, his eyes ugly. "Listen, Vernon! Don't give me any trouble! You're in this deeper than I am! You've got murder against you, as well as smuggling. If I'm ever exposed, you know that you and Sherry will both go down with me. What will your precious father think then, with his fine family pride and his bad heart?"

"Shut up!" Bob cried angrily. He leaped to his feet. "If it weren't for Dad, I'd kill you with my bare hands!"

"Really, Bob," Sherry said quietly, "perhaps we should talk this over. I'm not so sure that prison for both of us wouldn't be preferable to being married to Star."

Levitt's face went white and dangerous. "You're flattering," he said dryly, striving to retain his composure. "What, if I may ask, would have happened to Bob if I hadn't gotten him away from that mess and brought him here? The killing of Clyde Aubury was not any ordinary killing."

Aubury? Ross Haney's brows drew together, and he strained his ears to hear more.

"Yes, I think I should have earned your gratitude," Levitt continued. "Instead, I find you falling for that drifting cowhand."

Sherry Vernon's eyes lifted from her plate. "Star," she said coolly, "you could never understand through that vast ego of yours that Ross Haney is several times the man you could ever have been, even if you hadn't become a thief and a blackmailer of women."

Haney's heart leaped, and his lips tightened. In that instant, he would cheerfully have gone through the window, glass and all, and given his life if it would have helped. Yet even in his elation at her praise of him, he could not but admire the coolness and composure. Her manner was quiet, poised. He stared into the window, his heart pounding. Then she lifted her eyes and looked straight into his!

For an instant that seemed an eternity, their eyes held. In hers he saw hope leap into being, then saw her eyes suddenly masked, and she turned her head, passing something to her brother with an idle comment that ignored Levitt completely.

"Well," she said after a minute, her voice sounding just a tone louder, "everything is all right for the time. At least I have until Monday!"

He drew back. That message was for him, and between now and Monday was a lifetime—three whole days! Three days in which many things might be done, in which she might be taken from here—in which he might even kill Star Levitt. For he knew now that was what he would do if the worse came to the worst. He had never yet actually hunted a man down for the purpose of killing him, but he knew that was just what he would do if there was no other way out.

Tiptoeing to the corner of the house, Ross started for the stable and his horse, and then, as he stepped past the last tree, a huge cottonwood, a man stepped out. "Say, you got a match?"

It was Kerb Dahl!

Recognition came to them at the same instant, and the man let out a startled yelp and grabbed for his gun.

There was no time to grapple with the man, no chance for a quick, soundless battle. Too much space intervened so there was only one chance. Even as Dahl's hand grasped his gun, Haney plucked out his own gun and fired.

Flame stabbed from the muzzle, and then a second stab of fire. Dahl took a hesitant step forward, his gun half out. Then the gun belched flame, shooting a hole through the bottom of the holster, and Dahl toppled forward on his face.

Behind Dahl the bunkhouse door burst open, and there was a shout from the ranch house itself. As quickly Ross ducked around the stable and hit the saddle running.

The Appaloosa knew an emergency when he felt one and he lit out, running like a scared rabbit. A gun barked, then another, but nothing in that part of the country could catch the Appaloosa when he started going places in a hurry, and that was just what he was doing.

On the outskirts of Soledad, with the pounding hoofs of the pursuit far behind, Haney leaped the horse over a gully and took to the desert, weaving a pattern of tangled tracks into a trail where cattle had been driven, then cutting back into the scattered back alleys of Soledad, leaving town a few minutes later, crossing a shale slide and swinging around a butte to hit his old trail for Thousand Springs Mesa.

"Río, you saved my neck tonight, an' we took a scalp. I'd as soon never take another, but if we have to, let 'em all be *hombres* like Dahl."

Yet what was all this about a murder charge against Bob Vernon? And what was their connection with the smuggling and the cans of opium he had found in the cabin? He had known the smell the instant he lifted the can to his nostrils, for it is a smell one does not soon forget. He remembered it from a visit, a few years before, to some of the dives along the Barbary Coast. And now he must think. Somehow, some way, he must free Sherry from this entanglement, and as a last resort he would do it, if he must, by facing Star Levitt with a gun.

Chapter Fifteen

Haney's course was clear. Whatever other plans he might have had must be shelved and the whole situation brought into the open by Monday. Studying the situation carefully, he could see little hope, unless the sheriff and the investigating officers from the outside arrived on Monday. Then, if he could present his case—but Levitt would take every measure to avoid that and his only chance would be to get into town before time.

On Sunday night, in absolute blackness, the three rode down the back trail toward Soledad. Outside of town they slackened pace. Ross turned in his saddle as Burt and Mabry came up beside him.

He gestured toward the town. "It looks quiet enough. I'm going to leave my horse at May's. You two leave your horses there, too. Put them in the stable. Then you two hide out in the stable. I'm going first. You follow in a few minutes. I want to see Scott, and he'll go to Allan for me. If the worse comes to the worst, and there is no other way, I'm going gunning for Star. I'd rather die myself than see that girl forced to marry him, or to see him win after all this murder and deceit. However, I may give myself up when the sheriff gets here."

Mabry nodded thoughtfully. "Who are these *hombres* Levitt's bringin' in, Ross? Are they really the law?"

"Yeah, you see he calls Chubb the sheriff. Actually he's only a town marshal. The county seat is over a hundred miles away by trail, an' there's no deputy up here. Star Levitt is shrewd. He knows that sooner or later some word of this scrap will get out. Somebody, on a stage or somewhere, will talk. The chances are they already have. Well, so he sends to the governor for an investigating officer, wanting the whole thing cleared up. That puts him on the map as a responsible citizen. He'll do the talking and the men he selects will back him up, and the whole situation will be smoothed over. The chances are one of his men will be made a deputy sheriff. Then the investigatin' officers will go back to the capital and Levitt's in a nice spot. If any trouble comes up, they will always remember him, apparently rich, a stable citizen, a man who called on the law. They wouldn't believe a thing against him. His skirts will be clear, an' we three will be outlawed. Somehow, we've got to block that an' expose the true state of affairs."

"What is this joker you said you had?" Mabry asked.

"Wait. That will do for the showdown. Nobody knows about that but myself an' Scott. We'll have this whole show well sewed up."

He was the first to move forward, walking the

Appaloosa through the encircling trees to May Ashton's cabin on the edge of Soledad. There was no one in sight, but a light glowed in the cabin. He moved up and led his horse into the stable and left it there. Then he slipped along the wall of the house until he could glance into a window. The waitress was inside, and alone.

She opened the door at his tap, and he slipped inside. "You!" she gasped. "We were wondering how to get word to you. Star Levitt is marrying Sherry tomorrow."

"I know. What about the officers from the capital?"

"They'll be in tomorrow, too. In the morning. The sheriff is coming up from the county seat, and some attorney from the capital named Ward Clymer. Two state Rangers are coming with them. I've heard it all discussed in the restaurant."

"They will have a hearing? Where?"

"In the lobby of the hotel. It's the only place large enough, aside from the Bit and Bridle. I heard Voyle talking with Syd Berdue about it. Incidentally," she added quickly, "there's a warrant out for your arrest. Emmett Chubb has it. They want you for killing Kerb Dahl. Was that you?"

"Uhn-huh, but it was a fair shake. In fact, he went for his gun first. I had no choice but to shoot."

"Well, the order is out to shoot on sight, and they have Reward posters ready to go out tomorrow morning. They will be all over town for the officers to see when they come in. You're wanted for murder, dead or alive, and they are offering a thousand dollars."

Ross smiled wryly. "That will make it worse! A

thousand dollars is money enough to start the blood hunters out. Now, listen. I'm going to Scott, and I'm going now. Mabry and Burt will be in soon, and they'll hide here in the stable. They will be standing by in case of emergency. I'll try to communicate with you in case of really serious trouble, and then you can get word to them. I intend to give myself up to the officials and make them hold a preliminary hearing right here. I can talk them into that, I think. Then we can get facts in front of them."

"Ross, don't plan on anybody siding you," May said quickly. "Chubb has been around town with Hanson, and they have frightened everybody. You can't depend on a soul. I don't even know whether I'd have nerve enough to back you up, but I'm afraid Allan will. He's that kind."

The street was dark when Ross Haney stepped out of May's cabin. He did not try to keep out of sight, realizing that such an attempt, if seen, would be even more suspicious. He walked rapidly down the street, staying in the deep shadows, but walking briskly along. Scott was the man he must see. He must get to him at once, and he would know what to do. Also, it would be a place to hide.

Glancing across the street, he saw a half dozen horses standing at the hitch rail in front of the Bit and Bridle. There was light flooding from the windows, and the sound of loud laughter from within.

A man opened the door and stumbled drunkenly into the street, and for a moment Ross hesitated, feeling uneasy. The street was altogether too quiet; there was too little movement. He turned at right angles and went between a couple of buildings, starting for the back door of Scott's place. Once he thought he glimpsed a movement in the shadows, and hesitated, but, after watching and seeing nothing more, he went on up to the back door and tapped gently. The door opened, and he stepped in.

Scott glanced at him, and alarm sprang into his eyes.

"Set down," he said. "Set down. You've sure been stirrin' up a pile of trouble, Haney."

He poured a cup of coffee and placed it on the table. "Drink that," he said quietly. "It will do you good."

Scott stared at him as he lifted the cup. "Big trouble's goin' to break loose, Scott," Haney said. "I hope I can handle it."

His ears caught a subtle whisper of movement outside, and his eyes lifted, then his face went to a dead, sickly white.

Scott had a shotgun, and its twin barrels were pointed right at his stomach.

"Sit tight, son," he said sternly. "A move an' I'll cut you in two." He lifted his voice. "All right, out there! Come on in! I've got him!"

The door burst open and Emmett Chubb sprang into the room, and with him was Voyle, Tolman, and Allan Kinney!

Chubb's eyes gleamed and his pistol lifted. "Well, Mister Ross Haney, who's top dog now?"

"Hold it!" Scott's shotgun made a sharp movement. "You take her easy, Emmett Chubb! This man's my prisoner. I'm claimin' the reward, right now. Moreover, I'm holdin' him alive for Levitt!"

"You will not!" Chubb snarled. "I'll kill the dirty dog!"

"Not unless you want a blast from this shotgun!" Scott snapped. The old outlaw's blue eyes sparked. "Nobody's beatin' me out of my money! Kinney, here, he has a finger in it, maybe, because he tipped me off, but you take him away from me over my dead body!"

Baffled, Chubb stared from one to the other.

"He's right, Emmett," Kinney agreed. "He got him first."

Ross Haney stood flat-footed, staring from Kinney to Scott. "Sold out!" he sneered. "I might have suspected it!"

Kinney flushed, but Scott shrugged.

"A thousand dollars is a lot of money, boy. I've seen men killed for a sight less."

"Let's take him off to jail, then," Chubb said. "This ain't no place for him."

"He stays right here," Scott said harshly. "He's my prisoner until Levitt gets him, an' then Levitt can do what he's a mind to. Nobody's beatin' me out o' that money. Stay here an' help guard if you want, but don't you forget for one minute that he's my prisoner. This shotgun won't forget it."

Kinney slipped around behind Haney and lifted his guns. Reluctantly Haney backed into a corner and was tied to a chair. Shocked by the sudden betrayal, he could only stare from Allan to Scott, appalled by the sudden turn of fortune.

From the high, if desperate hopes of the day, he was suddenly smashed back into hopelessness, a prisoner, betrayed by the men he had most confidence in. How could they have known he was in town? There was only one way. May must have betrayed him! She and Allan must have planned together, and, when he left her house, she must have gotten word to him at once.

Chubb dropped into a chair and pulled one of his guns over into his lap. "I'd like to blast his heart out," he said sullenly. "What you frettin' so about, Scott? You get the money, dead or alive."

"Sure," Scott said. "And if you kill him, you'll lay claim to it. I wouldn't trust you across the street where that much money was concerned. Nor any of you." He chuckled, his eyes sneering at Haney. "Anyway, Levitt's top dog around here from now on, an' he's the boy I do business with. I'm too old to be shoved out in the cold at my time of life. I ain't figurin' on it. I'll work with Star, an' he'll work with me."

"I never heard of you bein' so thick with him." Chubb's irritation was obvious.

Scott chuckled. "Who got him into this country, do you suppose? I've knowed him for years! Who told him this place was right for a smart man? I did! That's who! Haney, here, he figured on the same thing. He figured on takin' over when Reynolds an' Pogue were out of it, but he was leavin' too much to chance. Star doesn't leave anything to chance."

Bitterly Ross Haney stared at the floor. This time he was finished. If Mabry and Burt had gone to May's, they would have been sold out, too. He listened, straining his ears for shots, hoping at least one of them would manage to fight it out and go down with a gun in his hand.

The situation was all Levitt's now. The man was a front rider, and these others were with him. He stared at Kinney, and the young man's eyes wavered and looked away. How could he have guessed that such a man would sell him out? And Scott? Of course, the old man was an admitted outlaw, or had been. Still, he had felt very close to the old man, and liked him very much.

There was no chance for Sherry now—unless. . . . His eyes narrowed with thought. What would they do with him? Would they get word to Star that he was a prisoner, then smuggle him out of town to be killed? Or would they bring him out in the open with evidence arrayed against him, or kill him trying to escape?

If only there would be some break, some chance to talk to Ward Clymer or the sheriff! Of course, held as a prisoner, with Reward posters out and stories Star and his men would tell, he would have himself in a bad position even before they talked to him, for they would be prejudiced against him, and everything he might say. And what evidence had he? Star Levitt would have plenty, and, as May had told him, no one in town would testify for him against Star. They were frightened, or they were getting on the bandwagon. He was through.

Unless—there was a vague hope—that Mabry and Burt had not been captured. If they could somehow free him? Knowing the manner of men they were, he knew they would not hesitate to make the attempt.

Chapter Sixteen

In the back room of the store the night slid slowly by and crawled into the gray of day, slowly, reluctantly. The rising sun found the sky overcast and no opening in the clouds through which it could shine down on the clustered, false-fronted frame buildings and adobes of Soledad. A lone Mexican, a burro piled twice its own height with sticks, wandered sleepily down the town's dusty street.

Pat walked out of the Bit and Bridle and stared at the sky, then turned and walked back within. A pump rattled somewhere, then began a rhythmical speaking.

Half asleep in his bonds, Ross Haney heard the water gushing into the pail in spouts of sound. He stirred restlessly, and his chair creaked. He opened his eyes to see four pairs of eyes leveled at him. Emmett Chubb, Voyle, Allan Kinney, and Scott all sat, ready and watchful. His lids fluttered and closed. Behind them his mind began to plan, to contrive.

No man is so desperate as a prisoner. No man so ready to plan, to try to think his way out. If only his hands were free! In a few minutes, an hour at most, the stage would rattle down the street and halt in front of the Cattleman's Rest Hotel and the passengers would go into the restaurant to eat. Later they might go upstairs to sleep. During that interval, he would know his fate. He touched a tongue to dry lips.

"Al," Scott said suddenly, "you take this here shotgun. I'll throw together a few ham an' eggs. I'm hungry as a hibernatin' bear in the springtime."

Tolman, who had left earlier, returned now and stuck his head in the door. "Stage a-comin'!" he said. "An' Syd Berdue just blowed in!"

"That VV bunch in yet?" Chubb asked, without turning his head. "When Dolph Turner gets in, you tell him about this. He'll see that Levitt knows first of all."

Scott was working around the stove and soon the room was filled with the pleasant breakfast smell of frying ham and eggs and the smell of coffee. Despite his worry, Haney realized he had been hungry, and for the first time recalled he had eaten nothing the night before.

Emmett Chubb got up. He was a stocky, swarthy man with a square jaw and a stubble of beard. His hair was unkempt, and, when he crossed the room to splash water on his face and hands, Ross noted his worn guns had notches carved in them, three on one gun, five on the other. Eight men.

"The only thing I'm sorry for," Chubb said as he dried his hands, his eyes on Haney, "is that I didn't get the chance to shoot it out with you in the street." His black eyes were sneering and cold. "I'd like to put you in the dust," he said. "I'd like to see you die."

"Well," Haney said dryly, "my hands are tied, so you're safe enough to try. You're a lot of yellow-backed double-crossers. You, Chubb, are a cheap murderer. You blew town fast enough after killin' Vin Carter or you'd have had a chance to draw on me . . . or run."

Chubb walked across the room and stopped, his feet apart, in front of Haney. Lifting his open palm, he slapped Ross three times across the mouth. Scott did not turn, and Kinney shuffled his feet on the floor.

"Maybe Levitt will give me the job," he said harshly. "I hope he does."

The door opened suddenly and three men stood there. Ross Haney's head jerked up as he saw Levitt. Star Levitt glanced from Chubb to Scott, and then indicated the men with him.

"Neal an' Baker, of the Rangers. They want the prisoner."

Chubb stared, disappointment and resentment struggling for place in his eyes. "Here he is. Scott's been holdin' him."

Neal bent over Haney and cut the ropes that tied his arms. "You come with us. We're havin' the hearin' right now."

Haney turned, and, as he started toward the door, he saw Scott smiling. The old outlaw looked right into his eyes and winked, deliberately. What did that mean?

Scowling, Haney walked across the street toward the hotel. Neal glanced at him a couple of times. "You know a man named Mabry?"

"Bill Mabry?" Ross turned to Neal, astonished. "Why, sure. He works for me, an' a mighty good man."

"When Clymer asks you questions," Neal said, "give him the information you have straight, honest, and without prejudice."

Puzzled by the suggestion, Ross Haney walked into the room, and was shown to a chair.

A big man with a capable, shrewd-looking face glanced at him sharply, then went back to examining some documents on the table. Several other men trooped in, and then Sherry and Bob Vernon walked into the room. More and more astonished, Ross stared from one to the other, trying to see what must have happened.

He had never believed that Levitt would allow Clymer to confront the Vernons, or himself, if it could be avoided. Yet here they all were, and it looked like a showdown. Allan Kinney was there, and May. The pretty waitress glanced at him, and he averted his eyes. Scott had come over, and Star Levitt was one of the last to come into the room.

From the dark expression on Levitt's face, he decided all could not be going well for the big man, and the thought cheered him. Anything that was bad news for Levitt was sure to be good news for him.

Ward Clymer sat back in his chair and looked over the room, his eyes noncommittal. "Now, friends," he said briskly, "this is an entirely informal hearing to try to clarify the events leading up to the battle between the Reynolds and Pogue factions and to ascertain the guilt, if any, of those who are here with us. Also," he glanced at Haney, "I am informed that Ross Haney, the cattleman, is held on a charge of murder for the slaying of one Kerb Dahl, a cowhand from the VV. If such is the truth, and if the evidence warrants it, Ross Haney will be taken south to the county seat for trial. In the meantime, let us examine the evidence.

"Mister Levitt, will you tell us the events that preceded the fight between Reynolds and Pogue?"

Star Levitt got to his feet, very smooth, very polished. He glanced around, smiled a little, and began. "It seems that before I arrived in the Ruby Hills country there had been considerable trouble over water and range rights, with sporadic fighting between the two big outfits. The VV, owned by the Vernons, was not involved in this feud, although there seemed to be some desire on the part of both outfits to possess the VV holdings and water. On the day the fight started there was some minor altercation over branding, and it led to a shooting which quickly spread until most of the hands on both sides were involved, with resulting deaths."

"What was your part in the fight?" Clymer asked shrewdly.

"None at all, sir. I saw trouble coming and withdrew my men and got out of the way myself. After it was over, we did what we could for the wounded."

"There are no witnesses present from the other outfits?"

"Oh, yes! Emmett Chubb, now the town marshal, survived the fight. Also Voyle, of the Box N, is here. Kerb Dahl, of the VV, who was in the middle of things was later murdered by the prisoner, Ross Haney."

"Sir?" Haney asked suddenly.

Clymer's eyes shifted to him, hesitated, and then asked: "Did you have a question?"

"Yes, I'd like to ask Star Levitt where his range holdings were."

"I don't see that the question has any bearing on the matter," Levitt replied coolly.

"It's a fair question," Clymer admitted. "It may have some later bearing on it. I understand you were running cattle. Where was your headquarters?"

Levitt hesitated. "On the VV," he said. "You see I am soon to marry Miss Vernon."

Clymer glanced curiously at Haney. "Does that answer your question?"

"Sure, it answers it for now. Only I want it plain to everybody that Star Levitt had no buildings on the range other than cattle and the use of the VV headquarters."

Levitt stared at Haney, and shrugged in a bored manner. The attorney then asked Chubb and Voyle a few questions about the killing, and through Scott, Pat, the bartender, and others brought out the facts of the long-standing feud between the Reynolds and Pogue outfits. Every story served to bolster Levitt's position. Bob Vernon offered his evidence in short, clipped sentences, and then Sherry hers.

As she started to return to her chair, Haney spoke up. "Another question. Sherry, did anyone warn you away from the roundup, telling you to leave at once, that there might be trouble?"

She hesitated. "Why, yes. Star Levitt did."

"I could see some of the men were spoiling for a fight," Star said quietly. "It seemed a bad place for a woman, due to the impending trouble and the profanity attending the work of the men."

"May I ask a few questions?" Ross asked.

"Mister Clymer," Levitt interrupted, "this man Haney is a troublemaker! His questions can do no good except to try to incriminate others and to put himself in a better light. The man is a murderer!"

Clymer shrugged. "We're here to ascertain the facts. However, the prisoner should be examined in connection with the killing of Kerb Dahl. What have you to say to that, Haney?"

"That it is impossible to divide the killing of Dahl from the other sides of the case. Nor is it going to be of any use to talk of it until the events leading up to that point are made plain."

"Well, that's reasonable enough," Clymer said. "Go ahead."

Levitt's lips tightened and his nostrils flared. Voyle had walked into the back of the room with Syd Berdue, and they stood there, surveying the crowd. With them was the silent man who had been Dahl's partner.

"I want to ask Levitt how many hands he had when he came into this country," Ross said evenly.

Star was puzzled and wary. "Why, not many. What difference does it make?"

"How many? You used the VV spread . . . how many hands did *you* have?"

"Why, one was actually all that came with me." The question puzzled Levitt and disturbed him. He couldn't see where it pointed.

"The one man was that short, dark man at the back of the room, wasn't it? The man called Turner?"

"That's right."

Haney turned suddenly in his chair and fired the question at Dahl's partner. "Turner, what's a piggin' string?"

"What?" The man looked puzzled and frightened. The question startled him, and he was irritated at being suddenly noticed.

"I asked what a piggin' string was. I'd also like to know what a grulla is."

Turner turned his head from side to side, eager for a way out, but there was none. He wet his lips with his tongue, and swallowed. "I don't know," he said.

"These questions make no sense at all!" Levitt said irritably. "Let's get on with the murder hearing!"

"They make sense to me," Ross replied. Then turning to Clymer, he added: "You, sir, were raised on a cow ranch, so you know that a piggin' string is a short piece of rope used to tie a critter when it's throwed . . . thrown. You also know that a grulla is a mouse color, a sort of gray, an' usually applied to horses. The point I'm gettin' at is that Levitt came into this country with one man who wasn't a cowhand. Turner doesn't know the first thing about a ranch or about cattle."

"What's that got to do with it?" Levitt demanded.

Clymer was looking at Ross Haney thoughtfully. He began to smile as he anticipated the reply.

"Why, just this, Levitt. How many cattle did you bring into this country?" Haney demanded sharply. He leaned forward. "An' how many have you got now?"

Somebody out in the room grunted and Scott was grinning from ear to ear. The question had caught Levitt flat-footed. Clymer turned on him, his eyes bright with interest. "A good question, Mister Levitt. On the way here you told me you ran a thousand head. Where did you get them?"

"That's got nothing to do with it!" Levitt shouted angrily. For the first time he was out in the open, and Ross Haney had led him there, led him by the nose into a trap. As Haney knew, when pushed, Levitt grew angry, and it was that he was playing for.

"Mister Clymer," Ross interrupted, "I think it has a lot to do with it. This man, claimin' to be a representative rancher, admits comin' into this country with one man who wasn't a cowhand even if he may be fairly good with a gun. No two men like that are bringin' in a thousand head of cattle into this country an' brandin' 'em. But I'll show you that Levitt does have a thousand head, or near to it, an' every one with a worked-over brand!"

"That's a lie!" Levitt shouted, leaping to his feet.

Ross settled back in his chair, smiling. "Now ask me about the killin' of Kerb Dahl," he said gently.

Star Levitt sagged back in his chair, flushed and angry. He had let go of his temper. Despite his burning rage, he knew he was in an ugly position where Haney, by his fool questions, had led him. The killing led away from the cattle, so he decided to jump at the chance.

Before he could speak, however, Clymer asked

Haney: "If he has the branded cattle now, who branded them?"

"Kerb Dahl, the man I killed on the VV, Voyle of the Box N, Tolman, who hired on after Levitt got here, an' Emmett Chubb, among others."

"That's absurd!" Levitt said contemptuously.

"Sherry, name the men you heard talking at Thousand Springs," Ross asked quickly.

The sudden question startled her, and, before Levitt could catch her eye, she glanced up and replied: "Why, Dahl was there, and Voyle, Tolman, and Sydney Berdue."

"What did they talk about?"

Levitt was leaning forward in his chair, his eyes upon her. Sherry glanced at him, and her eyes wavered. "Why, I. . . ." Her voice trailed off.

"Before you answer," Ross told her, "let me tell you that you've been the victims, you and your brother, of the foulest trick ever played." Haney turned to Clymer: "Sir, Miss Vernon was concealed near the springs and overheard some of the plotting between the men mentioned. These were the same men who altered the brands for Levitt. Through them Levitt engineered and planned the whole fight, forcing an issue between Reynolds and Pogue deliberately, and in the battle, killing the two men who opposed him in the Ruby Hills country. It will no doubt strike you that among the survivors of that battle were *all* the men seen by Miss Vernon at the springs. Also," he added, "Levitt was blackmailing the Vernons, using their ranch as a storage depot and transfer point for his deals in the opium trade."

Chapter Seventeen

Knocked off balance by these public revelations, Star Levitt struggled to his feet, his face ashen. The carefully planned coup was tumbling about his ears, and he who had come into the valley as a leader in a dope ring, and planned to become the legitimate owner of a great ranch, suddenly saw the whole thing reduced to chaos.

"Furthermore," Ross got to his feet, and the ringing sound of his voice reduced to silence the stir in the room, "I think this is the proper time to make a few points clear." Opening his shirt, he drew a leather wallet from inside it and from the wallet drew a handful of papers that he passed to Clymer. "Will you tell Mister Levitt," he said, "what you have there?"

Clymer glanced at them, then looked up in amazement. "Why, these are deeds!" he exclaimed, glancing from Haney to Levitt. "These indicate that you are the owner of both Hitson Springs and the Bullhorn ranch headquarters, including the water right. Also, here are papers that show Haney has filed on the Thousand Springs area!"

"What?" Star Levitt's fingers gripped the arms of his chair and his brow creased. Before his eyes came the whole plan he had made, all his planning, his actions—all were rendered perfectly futile. Who controlled the water in those three sources controlled the Ruby Hills, and there was no way of circumventing it. From the beginning he had been beaten, and now he had been made ridiculous.

"I told you," Haney said quietly, looking at Levitt, "that you had overlooked the obvious. Somehow a crook always does. Now, sir," Ross said to Clymer, "with the cattle brands I can show you, the evidence we can produce, I'd say that you have a strong case for robbery and murder against Star Levitt!"

There was a slight stir in the back of the room, and Haney's eyes shifted. Emmett Chubb was slipping from the room to the street.

As the accusation rang in the silent room, Star Levitt held himself taut. The crashing of his plans meant less to him now than the fact that he had been shown up for a fool by the cowhand he despised and hated. Suddenly the rage that was building within him burst into a fury that was almost madness. His face went white, his eyes glassy and staring, and, letting out a choking cry, he sprang for Haney.

Warned by Sherry's scream, Ross jerked his eyes back from the vanishing Chubb and lunged from where he stood, swinging two brain-jarring blows to the head. They rocked Levitt, but nothing could stop his insane rush, and Haney gave ground before the onslaught. Levitt swung wildly with both hands, beside himself with hate and fury.

But Ross lunged at him, burying a right in the bigger man's stomach, then hooking a powerful, jarring left to the chin. Levitt staggered and Ross, eager for battle, bulled into him, bringing his head down on Levitt's shoulder and smashing away with both hands in a wicked body attack. He threw the punches with all the power built into his shoulders by years of bulldogging steers and hard range work.

He caught Levitt with a wicked overhand right, and battered him back into the chairs. The crowd scattered. From somewhere outside Ross heard the sharp rap of a shot, and then another. Then quiet. His right smashed Levitt over a chair, and the big man came up with a lunge, grabbing for the chair itself.

Ross rushed him and Star tried to straighten, but Haney clubbed him with a fist on the kidney and the big man went to his knees. Ross stepped back, panting. "Get up!" he said. "Get up an' take it!"

Levitt lunged to his feet and Ross smashed his lips with a sweeping left. He ripped a gash in Levitt's cheek with a right. Star tottered back, his eyes glazed. He straightened then, shook his head, some measure of cunning returning to him. Suddenly he turned and hurled himself through the glass of the window!

Ross sprang to the window after him, and caught a fleeting glimpse of Emmett Chubb as a bullet whirred within a hair of his cheek and buried itself in the window frame. There was a clatter of horses' hoofs, then silence.

Haney's hands fell helplessly. Scott moved up beside him, handing him his guns. "Sorry I couldn't get 'em to you sooner," he said, "but you did plenty without 'em."

Clymer caught his arm. "You've loyal friends, Haney. Burt and Mabry stopped the stage outside of town. Levitt had ridden on ahead, and they took time to tell me a lot of things, and asked that I get you and the Vernons together with Levitt and withhold judgment until you had talked and I had listened. As it happens," he added, "Neal and I had both been reared on ranches where Mabry worked. We knew him for a good man, and an honest one. From the first we had doubts that all Levitt had told us was the truth. Mabry also had a cowhide with him, and any Western man could see the brand had been altered from a VV to Three Diamonds."

Ross shoved his guns into his holsters and pushed his way to Sherry who was standing, white and still, near the door, waiting for him. He said gently: "Sherry, we can talk about it some other time, but I think I can make a rough guess at most of it. Why don't you go in and get some coffee? I'll join you in a minute."

Mabry and Burt were waiting outside, and they had the Appaloosa. "We can chase 'em, boss," Rolly said, "but they've got quite a start."

"Later. I heard some shouting. What was it?"

"That was Voyle," Mabry said grimly. "He made a rush for his horse an' met Rolly halfway. He made a grab for his gun, an' I guess he wasn't as gun slick as he figured."

"Tolman?"

"Roped an' hog-tied. He'll go south with the Rangers, an', unless I miss my guess, he'll talk all the way. We've got Turner, too."

"Incidentally," Mabry added, "don't you jump to no conclusions about Kinney an' Scott. I ain't had much time to talk to Scott, but we moved down to May's like you said, an' all three of us seen you follered to Scott's by some of Levitt's crowd. They had us 'way outnumbered, an' Kinney came up and said if he butted in he might keep you from gettin' killed."

"That was my idea," Scott put in. "I thought I seen somethin' in the shadows when I let you in, an' I knowed I either had to get you as my prisoner or we'd both be in a trap. Chubb would kill you sure as shootin' if he got a chance, but as my prisoner I'd have the right to interfere."

"So, then Levitt, Chubb, an' Berdue are the only ones that got away?" Ross mused.

"Uhn-huh," Mabry agreed, and then, running his fingers through his coarse red hair, he commented: "That ain't good! I know that sort, an' you can take my word for it, they'll be back."

Yet as the days found their way down the year and the summer faded toward autumn, there was no further sign of the three missing men. The mornings became chill, but the sun still lay bright and golden upon the long valley, and the view from the growing house upon the mesa top changed from green to green and gold shot through with streaks of russet and deep red. The aspen leaves began to change and sometimes in the early morning the countryside was white with the touch of frost.

Rumors came occasionally to their ears. There had been a bank held up at Weaver, a stage had been looted and two men killed at Cañon Pass, and one of the three bandits had been recognized by a passenger as Emmett Chubb. Then the town marshal in Pie Town was shot down when he attempted to question a big, handsome man with a beard.

When Sherry rode the valley or over into the Ruby Hills, Ross Haney was constantly at her side, and the Appaloosa and Flame became constant companions. Despite the fact that no reports came of any of the three men being seen nearby, Haney was worried.

"Ross," Sherry said suddenly, "you've promised to take me to the crater in the lava beds. Why not today?"

He hesitated uneasily. "That place has me buffaloed," he said after a while. "I never go into it myself without wishing I was safely out. The way those big rocks hang over the trail scares a man. If they ever fell while we were in there, we'd never get out, never in this world."

She smiled. "At least we'd be together."

He grinned, and shoved his hat back with a quick, familiar gesture. His eyes twinkled. "That sure would be something, but I'd not like to have you confined in that place all your life. You might get tired of me. This way you can see a few folks once in a while an' maybe I'll wear better."

"But you've been there so many times, Ross, and

Rolly tells me it's perfectly beautiful. I want to see the ice caves, too."

Below them there was a faint rumbling and stirring within the mountain and they exchanged a glance. "I'm getting used to it now," he admitted, "but when I first heard it, that rumbling gave me the chills. When we move into the house, we'll have those holes fenced off. They are really dangerous."

"I know. Ever since you took me down there and showed me that awful hole, I've been frightened of it. Suppose someone was trapped down there, with a foot caught, or something? It would be frightful."

"It would be the end," Ross replied grimly. "When that geyser shoots up there, it brings rocks with it that weigh fifty or sixty pounds, and they rattle around in that cave like seeds in a gourd. You wouldn't have to have a foot caught, either. All you would have to do would be to get far enough away from the mouth of that cave so you couldn't make it in a few steps. A man wouldn't have a chance."

They were riding down the mesa through the slender aspens, their graceful white trunks like slender alabaster columns. The trail was carpeted with the scarlet and gold of autumn leaves.

"Somehow it all seems like some dreadful dream," she said suddenly. "We'd been so happy, Bob and I. It was fun on the ranch, working with the men, building our own place, learning all the new things about the West. Bob loved handling the horses and working with cattle, and then, when we were happiest, Star Levitt came out to the ranch. You can't imagine what a shock it was to us, for we thought all that had been left behind and forgotten.

Our brother, the oldest one in the family, had gone down to Mexico and got mixed up with a girl down there, and started using dope. He'd always been Father's favorite, and we all loved him, but Ralph was always weak and easily led. Levitt got hold of him, and used his name for a front to peddle dope in the States.

"Father has been ill for a long time with a heart condition that became steadily worse. He had just two great prides, two things to live for. One was his family reputation and the other was his children. Principally that meant Ralph. We knew about it, but we kept it from Dad, and later, when Ralph was killed down there, we managed to keep the whole truth of the story from him. We knew the shock and the disgrace would kill him, and, if by some chance he lived, he would feel the shame and the disgrace so much that his last years would be nothing but sorrow.

"Star told us that he needed our ranch. It was the proper working base for him, not too far from Mexico, yet in easy reach of a number of cities. He said he wanted to use the ranch for a headquarters for two months, and then he would leave. If we did not consent, he threatened to expose the whole disgraceful affair and see that my father heard it all. We were foolish, of course, but it is so hard to know what to do. And Levitt didn't give us time. He just started moving in. The next thing we knew he had his own men on the ranch and we were almost helpless. Reynolds and Pogue were outlaws or as bad, and we could not turn to them. There was nobody, until you came."

Ross nodded grimly. "Don't I know it? When I

started digging into the background of this country, I found less good people here than anywhere I ever knew. And the best folks were all little people."

"It was after he had been here a few weeks," Sherry continued, "that he decided to stay. He was shrewd enough to know he couldn't keep on like that forever, and here was a good chance to have power, wealth, and an honest income. He saw the fighting between the Box N and RR was his chance."

The two rode on in silence, their horses' hoofs making little sound on the leaf-covered trail. Suddenly, before Ross realized how they were riding, they were at the entrance to the lava bed trail.

Sherry laughed mischievously. "All right, now. As long as we're here, why don't we go in? We can be back before dark, you told me so yourself."

He shrugged. "All right, have it your own way."

Chapter Eighteen

Very reluctantly the Appaloosa turned into the narrow trail between the great black rolls of lava. Once started, there was no turning back, for until a rider was well within the great cleft itself, there was insufficient room for any turning of the horses.

When they reached the deepest part of the crevasse, where in some bygone age an earthquake or volcanic eruption had split the rim of the crater deep into the bedrock, Ross pointed out the great crags suspended over the trail.

"This place will be inaccessible someday," he told her. "There will be an earthquake or some kind of a jar, and those rocks will fill the cleft, so there will be no trail or place for one. From the look of them, a man might get them started with a bar or lever of some kind. I never ride in here without getting the creeps at the thought. They are just lying up there, and all they need is the slightest start, and they would come roaring and tumbling down."

Tilting her head back, Sherry could see what he meant, and for the first time she understood something of the fear that Ross had of this place. One enormous slab that must have weighed hundreds of tons seemed to be hanging, ready to slide at the slightest touch. It was an awesome feeling to be riding down here, with no sound but the *click* of their horses' hoofs, and to have those enormous rocks poised above them.

Yet once within the crater itself, she forgot her momentary fears in excitement over the long level of green grass, the running water, and the towering cliffs of the crater that seemed to soar endlessly toward the vast blue vault of the sky. Great clouds piled up in an enormous mass in the east and north, seeming to add their great height to the height of the cliffs.

It was warm and pleasant in the sunlight, and they rode along without talking, listening to the lazy sound of the running water, and watching the movements of the few remaining great red and brindle cattle that were becoming more tame due to the frequency of visits.

Haney said: "There must have been more than six hundred down here, and probably would have been more, but there are a good many varmints around. I've seen cougars down here, an' heard 'em."

"Where are the ice caves?" Sherry demanded. "I want to see them. Rolly was telling me about the crystals."

For two hours they rambled on foot over the

great crater and in and out of the caves. They found several where cattle and horses had been drinking, and whatever cattle they found, they started back toward the trail. Then suddenly, as they were about to leave, Sherry caught Haney's arm. "Ross!" There was sudden fear in her voice. "Look!"

It was a boot track, small and quite deep. Her breath caught. "It might be . . . Rolly!" Her voice was tight, her fear mounting.

"No, it wasn't Rolly." Mentally he cursed himself for ever bringing her here. "That foot is smaller than either Mabry's or Burt's, an' a heavy man made it. Let's get out of here."

When they were outside, he could see the pallor of her face in the last of the sunlight. He glanced at the sky, surprised at the sudden shadows although it was drawing on toward evening. Great gray thunderclouds loomed over the crater, piling up in great, bulging, ominous clouds. It was going to rain, and rain hard.

Leading the way, he started for the horses, every sense alert and wary, yet he saw no one. His movements started the cattle drifting again, and, as they reached the horses, he told her, glancing at the sky: "You go ahead. I think I'll start the rest of the cattle out of here while I'm at it."

"You can't do it alone," she protested.

"I'll try. You head for home now. You'll get soaked."

"Nonsense! I have my slicker, and. . . ." Her voice faded and her eyes fastened on something beyond Ross's shoulder, widening with fear and horror.

He knew instantly what it was she saw, and for a fleeting moment he considered making his draw as he turned, but realized the girl was directly in the line of fire.

"And so, after so long a time, we meet again!" The voice was that of Star Levitt. But there was a strange tone in it now, less of self-assurance and something that sounded weirdly like madness, or something akin to it.

Carefully Ross Haney turned and met the eyes that told him the worst. All the neatness and glamour of the man was gone. The white hat was soiled, his shirt was dirty, his face unshaven. His eyes were still the large, magnificent eyes, but now the light of insanity was in them. Haney realized the line between sanity and something less had always been finely drawn in this man. Defeat and frustration had been all that was needed to break that shadow line.

"Oh, this is great!" Levitt chortled. "Today we make a clean sweep! I get you, and later, Sherry! And while I am doing that, Chubb and Berdue will finish off Mabry and Burt. They are up on the mesa now, waiting for them!"

"On the mesa?" Haney shrugged. "They'll never surprise the boys there. Whenever one of us has not been on the mesa all day, we are very careful. We've been watching for you, Levitt."

Star smiled. "Oh, have you? But we found our own hiding place. We found a cave there, an ideal spot, and that's where they'll wait until they can catch Mabry and Burt without warning them."

"A cave?" Ross repeated. Horror welled up within him and he felt the hackles rising along his neck and his scalp prickled at the thought. "A cave? You mean you've been in that cave on the mesa?"

Levitt smiled. "Only to look, enough to know that it was an ideal hiding place. At first, I planned to stay, too, but then, when I saw you two leaving the mesa and heading for the lava beds, I decided this was a better chance. Besides"—he glanced at Sherry—"I want her for a while . . . alone. She needs to be taught a lesson."

Ross Haney stared at him. "Levitt, you're mad. That cave where those men are hiding is a death-trap. If they aren't within a few feet of the opening, they won't have a chance to get out of there alive. Did you see that black hole in the center? That's a geyser. Those men will be trapped and drowned."

Levitt's smile vanished. "That's a lie, of course. If it isn't, it won't matter. I was through with them, anyway. And Mabry and Burt are small fry. It is you two that I wanted."

Ross Haney had shifted his position slightly now and he was facing Levitt. His heart was pounding, for he knew there was only one chance for them. He must draw, and he must take a chance on beating Levitt to the shot. He would be hit, he was almost sure, but regardless of that he must kill Star Levitt.

Wes Hardin had beaten men to the shot several times when actually covered with a gun. There were others who had done it, but he was no fool, and knew how tremendously the odds weighed against him. Thunder rumbled and a few spatters of rain fell.

"Better get your slicker, Sherry," he said calmly. "You'll get wet."

His eyes were riveted upon Star Levitt, but what he waited for happened. As the girl started to move, Levitt's eyes flickered for a fraction of an instant, and Ross Haney went for his gun.

Levitt's gun flamed, but he swung his eyes back and shot too fast, for the bullet ripped by Haney's head just as Ross flipped the hammer of his gun.

Once! Twice! And then he walked in on the bigger man, his heart pounding, Levitt's gun flaming in his face, intent only upon getting in as many shots as possible before he was killed.

A bullet creased his arm and his hand dropped. Awkwardly he fired with his left-hand gun, and knew the shot had missed, yet Star Levitt, his shirt dark with blood, was wilting before his eyes, his body fairly riddled with the bullets from Haney's first, accurate shots.

Ross held his gun carefully, then fired again, and the shot ripped away the bridge of Star's nose, smashing a blue hole in his head at the corner of his eye.

Yet Star wouldn't go down. The guns wavered in his hands, then as his knees slowly gave away, some reflex action brought the guns up. Both of them bellowed their defiance into the pouring rain, their flames stabbing, then winking out. As the echoes of the gunfire died, there was only the rain, pouring down into the crater like a great deluge.

Sherry rushed to him. "Oh, Ross! You're hurt! Did he hit you?"

He turned dazedly. He didn't feel hurt. "Get into

that slicker!" he yelled above the roar of the rain. "We've got to pull out of here! Think of those rocks in this rain, and the lightning! Let's go!"

Fighting his way into his slicker, he saw the girl mount, and then he crawled into the saddle. The cattle moved when he started his horse toward them. Suddenly he made a resolution. He was taking them out—now.

Surprisingly the big steer that took the lead seemed to head into the cleft of his own choice, or possibly because it seemed to offer partial shelter from the sweep of the rain, or perhaps because he had seen so many of his fellows go that way in the weeks past.

Waving the girl ahead of him, Ross followed on into the cleft, casting scared glances aloft at the huge rocks. "Get on!" he yelled. "Get going!"

He glanced up again as they neared the narrowest part. He grabbed a stone and hurled it at a loitering steer, and the animal sprang ahead.

Sherry cast a frightened look upward and her eyes widened with horror. Her face went stark white as though she had been struck.

A thin trickle of stones fell, splashing into the cleft. A steer ahead stopped and bawled complainingly, and Ross grabbed a chunk of rock from the bank and hurled it, and the steer, hit hard, struggled madly to get ahead.

Sherry moved suddenly, closing up the gap between her horse and the nearest cattle, harrying them onward with stones and shouts. Ross looked up again, and, caught as in a trance, he saw the great slab stir ponderously, almost majestically. Its table-like top inclined, and then slowly, but with gathering impetus, it began to slide!

Shale and gravel rattled down the banks, and Ross touched spurs to his horse. The startled Appaloosa sprang ahead, forcing Flame into the steers, that began to trot, and then, as the two horses crowded up into the folds of lava but out of the cleft in the crater wall, the air behind them was suddenly filled with a tremendous sound, a great, reverberating roar that seemed to last forever.

The rain forgotten, they sat, riveted in place, listening to the sound that was closing the crater forever, and leaving the body of Star Levitt as the only thing that would ever tell of human movement or habitation.

Yet as they remembered what Star Levitt had said about Berdue and Emmett Chubb, they unconsciously moved faster, and once out of the lava beds they left the cattle to shift for themselves and turned toward the mesa trail.

There was no let-up to the rain. It roared down in an increasing flood. They bowed their heads and hunched their slickers around them. The red of Flame's coat turned black with wet. Under his slicker, Ross rode with one hand on his gun, hoping for no trouble, but searching every clump of brush, every tree.

Rolly Burt ran from the cabin and grabbed their horses when they swung down. "Hustle inside an' get dry!" he yelled. "We've been worried as all get-out!"

When they got inside and had their slickers off, Mabry looked up, rolling a smoke. "Burt thought he saw Chubb today. We were worried about you."

"You haven't seen them?" Ross turned on him sharply.

Burt came in, overhearing the question. "No, an' I'm just as well satisfied. Say"—he looked up at them—"that danged geyser sure gives off some funny noises! I was over close when it sounded off the last time this afternoon, and I'd've swore I heard a human voice a-screechin'! That's one reason we have been worried about you two, although Bill did say you rode off the mesa."

Sherry's face blanched and she turned quickly toward an inner room.

Rolly stared after her. "Hey, what's the matter? Did I say something wrong?"

"No, just forget about it. And don't mention that geyser again." Then Ross explained, telling all that had happened during the long, wet afternoon, the end of Star Levitt, and the closing of the great cleft.

Sherry came out as they finished speaking. "Ross, those poor men. I hated them, but to think of anything human being caught in that awful place."

"Forget about it. They asked for it, and now it's all over. Look at that fire! It's our fire, in our own fireplace. Smell that coffee Mabry has on. And listen to the rain. That means the grass will be growin' tall an' green next year, honey, green on our hills an' for our cattle!"

She put a hand on his shoulder, and they stood there together, watching the flames dance, listening to the fire chuckling over the secrets locked in the wood, and hearing the great drops hiss out their anguish as they drowned themselves in the flames. A stick fell, and the blaze crept along it, feeling hungrily for good places to burn. From the kitchen they heard the rattle of dishes and the smell of bacon frying, and Rolly was pouring the coffee.

About the Editor

Jon Tuska is the author of numerous books about the American West as well as editor of several short story collections, BILLY THE KID: HIS LIFE AND LEGEND (Greenwood Press, 1994) and THE WESTERN STORY: A CHRONOLOGICAL TREASURY (University of Nebraska Press, 1995) among them. Together with his wife Vicki Piekarski, Tuska co-founded Golden West Literary Agency that primarily represents authors of Western fiction and Western Americana. They edit and co-publish forty titles a year in two prestigious series of new hardcover Western novels and story collections, the Five Star Westerns and the Circle ⓋWesterns. They also co-edited the ENCYCLOPEDIA OF FRONTIER AND WESTERN FICTION (McGraw-Hill, 1983), THE MAX BRAND COMPANION (Greenwood Press, 1996), THE MORROW ANTHOLOGY OF GREAT WESTERN SHORT STORIES (Morrow, 1997), and THE FIRST FIVE STAR WESTERN CORRAL (Five Star Westerns, 2000). Tuska has also been editing an annual series of short novel collections, STORIES OF THE GOLDEN WEST, of which there have so far been six volumes.